A.D. Sui
THE DRAGONFLY GAMBIT
Neon Hemlock Press

NEON HEMLOCK

Neon Hemlock Press
www.neonhemlock.com
@neonhemlock

The Dragonfly Gambit
A.D. Sui

Cover Illustration by Katherine Lam
Cover Design and Layout by dave ring
Interior Design and Layout by dave ring
Edited by dave ring

Print ISBN-13: 978-1-952086-79-3
Ebook ISBN-13: 978-1-952086-80-9

THE DRAGONFLY GAMBIT

BY A.D. SUI

To me, and to all the angry women who made me.

If you're listening to this,

        then we have arrived at our ends.

We kept our promises as women of our constitution should. I have ended the twenty-year-long uprising against the Rule in just six months, just as you've asked of me. And you, the Third Daughter of the Rule, Eternal Rightful, both beautiful and deadly, have ended me. Regrettably, this means I wasn't there to witness the instance when your façade came down, when all control seeped through your fingers.

Alas, we were never meant to live in the future we were carving from the decaying carcass of your empire.

Now you can rest. We can both rest. We did the best with what we had.

THE OPENING

ONE

BY ALL ACCOUNTS, I should be scared.

Intelligence and Investigations boys are overzealous. They like to break things: doors, people, entire local governments if they get the chance. Five more flights of stairs until they're at my door. After three weeks of stealthily tracking me, taking shifts to shoot unflattering photographs from the flashing billboard across the street, my day of reckoning is finally here.

I can't complain. It's nice to feel wanted.

They pass from one glowing screen to the next, slithering along the chipped walls. Their silhouettes scurry up the stairwell, tasers drawn, back-to-back, like they're in some sort of an active shooter situation. The cameras I set up in the months prior are paying for themselves. Who's the paranoid one now?

Shay will do the knocking. He's here to ease the blow. Ten years ago we were friends, in the way where you know how the other sleeps, in the way where I know he's about to puke by the way he stops talking. He arrived not a full cycle ago to close the deal, I'm sure.

When he knocks, it's an official rattle, the sort that lets you know you're in trouble, the sort that's followed by a black bag over your face and a trip to an undisclosed site. Shay knocks like he carries the authority of the Rule with him, like it will back him up on any decision. Little does he know, the Rule will break him just as well, if necessary.

I limp over to answer.

"You're not a delivery bot." I give him a sour smile. Shay is stiff as a board, his own taser unholstered. He strategically avoids staring at my bare chest, or the rest of my naked body. The slumped shoulder and the hoisted arm, far too atrophied to look functional.

"Nez, I'm on orders to retrieve you."

"That's no way to greet an old friend, *Captain*."

"Don't make this harder than it needs to be. I have guys in every stairwell, armed, ready to take you out."

"On a date, I gather?"

"Don't be difficult. Be glad I knocked."

"Be glad I didn't blow you to bits while you were climbing the stairs."

Shay's face darkens for a moment. Okay, the cameras *and* the traps are paying for themselves. He retraces the stairwell, his eyes darting from left to right as he replays his ascent in slow motion. Every turn, every step. "Third floor?"

"Third floor."

Shay rocks his weight anxiously between his feet, pretending not to notice the projected hologram and the floating code behind me. "Look—" he says, visibly uncomfortable. "We gotta get moving, so, you need to put something on. The guys—they're—"

I disappear into my apartment and Shay follows like an oversized puppy. He steps cautiously over a box of moldy takeout. I bet he gets danger pay any time he docks on any non-central planet. "This wasn't my idea," he says, and I've never wanted to punch him more. Not his idea. When was the last time he *had* an idea?

Investigation and Intelligence has him dressed to the nines. In his grey uniform and gold cuffs, Shay is a walking, talking propaganda poster. The jawline helps. No wonder him and Kaya—no, there's no sense going there.

While I saunter around the room, Shay stands awkwardly in the center. His pin camera is recording from his chest, so this conversation will remain lukewarm. "If it were up to me, I'd leave you alone, but the Rule needs you."

"The Rule doesn't need *me*, it needs a way to turn a stalemate."

Shay flinches. "Nez."

"*I* said it, not you."

"I should correct you. The Rule is not in a stalemate. The Rule is winning."

I throw a shirt in Shay's general direction. "It's been *winning* for twenty years now."

Every empire falls. You can kick and scream, and whine, and plead, but every empire will have its fall. The Rule has been doing well for over a thousand years, expanding at an impossible rate, absorbing small and medium system-level governments into itself. Sometimes peacefully. Mostly not. But it got too big, and the edges began to fray. Shay knows this. Anyone with half a brain knows it. It took a few hundred years for systems to actively rebel and break away. It took less than a decade for full-out war to ignite after that. That was twenty years ago, and the Rule has yet to reclaim the systems. Two generals have already fallen, the First and the Second Daughters. The Third doesn't have much time left either.

"Safe to assume you're not going to tell me where we're headed?"

Shay affirms with a shake of his head. What a good little soldier.

I find a passably clean shirt and shove it over my head. My left arm goes in elbow first, and then inertia takes it the rest of the way. If I flail too much my shoulder will pop out. You gotta learn to get around these things if you want to get by on your own.

"Nez, something more substantial, *please.*"

I'm willing to put just as much effort into my appearance as the Rule did into summoning me. I slide on my pants with my right hand, do them up. I take a sharpened pencil and plunge it through my hair, twist it around and stab through the bun.

Shay watches the entire routine silently. Then, when I'm done, he half-heartedly asks, "How's the—"

He means the arm. Everyone *always* means the arm. He fails to acknowledge the limp, the slight toe drag, the way my left eyelid never fully opens, the upward curve of my lip. The devil is in the details. Shay could never even begin to comprehend the extent of the damage. Just one ruptured vertebra and any dreams of piloting anything other than a desk are gone. *Poof!* I shrug at Shay with my right shoulder. "It's fine, won't get in the way of whatever it is you want me for, I'm sure."

Shay gestures out of my apartment and down the long, shadowy corridor I've crawled through many times, too drunk to stand. He's a real gentleman, and as of a man of such constitution, he lets me wrap up my projected code and schematics before we leave. By which I mean he lets me "accidentally" pour a litre of coffee on the CPU while he turns his back and politely stares out into the hallway. I watch it fizzle and die without making any small talk. Then, he leads me down the corridor and into the stairwell, where I'm greeted by the wrong end of a rifle.

"Down," Shay says, and the boy in dark grey coveralls lowers the muzzle.

"There's a transport waiting for us downstairs. You will be hooded and handcuffed, and taken to an undisclosed site." I'd really hoped we could do without the undisclosed sites. "Don't bother staying awake, it's a long trip. You can ask for a sedative once you're inside, I highly recommend it." Shay slips into the Intelligence persona as easily as a snake into a rabbit's burrow. Ten years and the Rule still has him running errands like a recruit—either Shay's gone and royally fucked up or this is important to the Third Daughter.

"For once I'll stay sober." We start down the stairwell, boy-with-rifle ahead of me, Shay behind me. I'd be stupid to make a run for it. I haven't run in nearly a decade, today would be hell of a day to start.

"Rule Eternal," Shay greets the driver once we're outside. A sleek, black transport has been bestowed upon me, the interior of which I will never see. Shay pulls a hood out of thin air. "You know the drill."

"Wait—"

In the early hours of the day, suns still safety tucked beyond the horizon, the rain lashes frigid droplets against the exposed parts of me. If I tilt my face skywards, it patters against my eyelids, my lips. I can taste the acidity as the water seeps into the corners of my mouth.

"What are you doing?" Shay looms over me, impatiently.

"I have a feeling this is the last time I'll see rain," I tell Shay and let him pull the black-out fabric of the hood over my face. Immediately, it's difficult to breathe. It's going to be a long ride.

Shay slips inside the car beside me. He presses cold steel to my wrists and at once they are bound and immobile. Based on the sounds of shuffling, there are four of us in the car. I manage to keep my mouth shut for what feels like an hour. "What does the Third Daughter want me with?"

"What makes you think it's the Third Daughter?"

Oh, I don't know. Maybe it's because if this was an Intelligence and Investigations solo assignment, I'd be missing half my fingernails by now? "Let me take a gander." Sometimes, I really need to keep my mouth shut. "The Rule is at a stalemate. You've pushed your tech as far as it will go and it gave you, what? A marginal advantage? One that you wasted because the breakaways have much better pilots? You're matched in tech and now you want someone like me to come in and fix this problem for you, you want an edge, you want—"

Shay stabs me with a sedative. *Rude.* The last I remember is the artificially melodic launch countdown , and then everything disappears into a chemically induced black-out.

HANDS.

There are hands on me, and I have no energy to fight them off. Strong hands. *Cold.* They're moving me. Somewhere? Moving me up? Where is up anyway? Someone shines a blinding light into my eye.

"Stay still." A commanding voice comes from above and I obey by habit. I just can't rinse the soldier out, no matter how much I try. The sedative keeps the panic at bay. My heart rate never goes past seventy.

"Buy me a drink first," I slur, and the world disappears around me.

SHAY HANDS ME a plastic sippy cup filled with sweet juice of an unknown variety.

"I don't blame you, you know," I say, still slurring. Oh no, what am I replying to? "All of us had to find ways to survive. You found yours in uniform. I don't take it personally."

Shay watches with wary eyes and nods along. Whatever sedative knocked me out must have produced hints of unwanted amnesia. My brain started recording only now, but we could have been chatting for hours. Oh *no.* The room is anything but cozy. A two-way mirror shimmers in the dim lights and there are at least four cameras by the ceiling that I can count. Five, if you include the pin camera on Shay's chest.

I flex my legs and drive my heels into the floor. Wherever we are now, we're not planetside. Shay has given me magnetic soles and left my arms uncuffed.

This just might be more of a conversation than a beating.

"Now that we've put some distance behind us, let's have a chat," Shay says. Detached. Professional.

I nod along as I tense various parts of my body to test their function. Looks like the sedative is the only thing that was used. They transported me in a rush, probably unconscious; my left shoulder aches as if I've been laying on it for too long. I have yet to piss myself, but honestly, I'm not even sure I'm wearing the same pants as when I left my apartment. Which, by these estimates, puts us between six and eight hours travel time. With an extra half an hour to throw my unconscious body like a sack of potatoes on and off shuttle, I'd say we're halfway to the frontlines.

Normally, I'd agree that everything they've done to me so far was a well-deserved consequence to my actions (the usual: sabotage, treason, I dabble in a few), but the lack of actual consequences is unnerving.

"I wouldn't go as far as to say it was treason," Shay says. "Broadcasting the details of Vice-Admiral Treped's divorce to every station that would listen hardly constitutes a crime against the Rule, although I did find it highly entertaining." He grins and I break into a sweat at how little control I have over keeping my thoughts inside my head where they belong.

Shay's aware of this. "You've been busy since we last saw each other."

Yes, I wasn't exactly sitting there twiddling my thumbs for a decade.

"You developed shield-penetrating drones, you obtained and revealed classified locations of the major fleet operations, you shut down payroll on three major Rule carriers, and of course—" Shay raises his eyebrows, "—you managed to leak fighter schematics to the breakaways."

"They had those already. First Daughter herself armed the annexed systems."

"I don't believe that to be true."

But the thing about the truth is that you don't have to believe in it for it to still be the truth. Truth shouldn't bend to favouritism. One such truth is that the Oran system, my home, faithfully adhered to the assimilation agreement, allowing their children to be conscripted for the Rule's fleet as long as the system itself was allowed to maintain some of its governing power. Shay, Kaya, and yes, me, ended up in the Rule's ranks thanks to that requirement. That is a truth. One, I begrudgingly accept.

Once there were suspicions that Oran might break away from the Rule, all assimilation agreements were thrown out. The entire system, all fifteen planets that comprised it, was vaporized sometime before I was discharged. It wasn't personal, just like Shay coming to collect me wasn't personal. This is also a truth I must accept. Kaya and Shay continue to serve despite what happened to our home. I still struggle with that one.

"We're not here for the First Daughter," I say.

"We're here to put an end to pointless fighting."

"Oh, has the Third Daughter decided to surrender?"

A faint smile flickers across Shay's lips. "Nez—" he warns.

The air grows thick between us, and I brace for a thunderstorm. "I'm not going to help you optimize your baby killing."

The sudden pain is blinding. It twists my insides with an iron claw as I double over and hurl all over my pants. Then, hurl again on to the floor. When my vision returns, my forehead presses against the metal table and there's rust in my mouth. I force a laugh. "When did you implant that?" There's a shaved patch at the nape of my neck which also happens to be the epicenter of the pain.

There's no answer. A second shock shatters my world. Something about where the implant sits in my neck causes it to impact the left side more than right. My arm convulses with bone-shattering strength. Luckily, my stomach is empty and I just dry heave until the shock passes. "Oof" is all I can manage.

Shay swivels in his chair, back and forth, like a bored toddler. "Years away from any real action have made you soft, Nez." He leans over and gives me a pat on the shoulder. "Don't forget, you were once a baby-killer in training too, eager to see some baby-killing action. Don't get all high and mighty. The Third Daughter doesn't need, nor want your loyalty or any sort of change of heart, she simply wants you to optimize our fighters."

"Shock me all you want," I pause to spit out a piece of protein I ingested two days ago (three? Time is weird right now), "but you've pushed your fighter tech to its limit. There's nothing more I can do. You won't squeeze much else out of it." Or me. I promise you there's nothing more left of me.

Shay shrugs. The creases around the corners of his eyes weren't there when we last saw one another. We share in the damp silence, inhaling the putrid smell wafting from the floor. "Well," he says at last, with a wistful smile "you do have a talent for making something out of scraps. Try and apply yourself. The Third Daughter might have a gentle hand compared to her sisters, but Intelligence and Investigations tends to correct for that."

He leaves me alone then, with the puddle of bile and the contents of my stomach on the floor, and if I could, I'd cry, but there's nothing in my stomach, not to mention the rest of me. For the first time in what I think is two days, there is a moment of silence, of reprieve. And I wish for nothing more than it to end. I dig my nails into my forearm, but the pain barely registers. One fucking vertebra. One vertebra bursting was enough to end a career, enough to end a future.

But then what kind of future would it have been, flying for the Rule?

I shouldn't blame Kaya for what happened, but I do. Kaya.

Kaya Laux. The Iron Fox, the ace of the Rule, the best fighter pilot in the galaxy—supposedly, according to the Third Daughter and to the millions of propaganda posters around any space port. But it wasn't always like that. She wasn't always spewing militant garbage from an impersonal hologram, the face of the Rule's fleet, a million miles away.

I rest my head against the table again. No matter how tightly I shut my eyes, the world spins. No, she used to be much closer. The door opens and even without raising my head I can tell that Shay is back for me.

"Time to go," he says, cold and rehearsed, just as they taught him in the academy and enforced through years of service. Money well spent.

I have a feeling he won't let me change. "Will Kaya be there?"

"Don't worry about that right now."

I take it as a *yes*.

TWO

THE PROBLEM WITH military hangars is that they are designed to withstand a direct hit from a nuclear warhead and yet, no one has the mind to reinforce and improve the very soft people that inhabit them. People that easily perish from the tiniest stab wound or drink of contaminated water. The dichotomy has begun to bother me for a reason I've yet to place. Maybe I'm getting too introspective in my age. People are soft and fallible; people start wars they don't have the strength or endurance to win. Maybe it's the softness that bothers me after all, the sheer waste of it all.

This particular hangar belongs to the Rule's flagship, which is barely two gate-jumps away from the frontlines. The ship sits in a cluster with five other cruisers, and a handful of smaller vessels, waiting for a golden chance at a counter-offensive. People, rations, ammunition, even the shocker in my brainstem are all delivered here from their manufacturing sites on Rule colonies. The Rule itself makes nothing except for war. I'm not supposed to say any of this out loud, of course. The fact that I even know it is probably what got me in this mess to begin with.

Shay is still by my side, wearing fresh-pressed blues against all odds. He must have shaved and eaten while I was asleep on the cot the Rule so kindly provided (bless the Rule Eternal). I think I ate. Yesterday's assault on my brain has severely impacted my short-term memory.

I've been issued a pair of standard issue blues with no insignia on them. Here, I have no rank. Not anymore. I pull my collar away and take a sniff. I must have also showered at some point. With the two middle buttons undone, I drape my arm through the hole and into the makeshift sling. Good enough to relieve the tension.

The walls of the hanger curve all the way to the ceiling and I have to crane my neck at a painful angle to follow their silhouette all the way to where they end. Kaya's eyes follow me from the hundreds of posters plastered around the hangar. In the most egregious, she is seductively propped up against her fighter, helmet in hand. The text reads *Invest in Our Daughters, Invest in the Future!* Another is a close-up of her face that reads *Ready! Fire! Victory!*

I might just puke again.

Hundreds of fighters line the floor, indiscernible grey against grey. Ignoring both Shay and I, thousands scurry between charging stations, pilots in black flight suits and techs in their brown coveralls. There are faces from all of the Rule here, joined together by the very conscription requirements that brought Shay and myself into the fleet. I can pick out a few native to Oran, techs mostly. They chat amongst themselves in a language I can no longer understand, that neither Shay, nor I, nor Kaya can understand. Still, I dream of it, singing songs I make no meaning of.

The Rule makes nothing. It only takes. Shay blends in effortlessly, like he's molted everything Oran from himself.

Out of the three of us, he had the least trouble shortening the vowels of his speech, adopting the right diction. Speaking the right way, eating the right way, the oval of his face, the lightness of his hair make it easy for him to blend in with the central residents. Although, anywhere in the Rule, from the blinding center to the perpetually frozen outposts everyone avoids an Intelligence uniform.

I give a long whistle to get Shay's attention.

"What?" He frowns.

I tilt my head upwards until I lose my balance and stagger backwards like a dumb bird. "They didn't make them this big in our day."

Shay *hmms* in agreement and extends his arm in the direction of the middle lane of fighters. "This way." Even with me, he never points. Pointing is *aggressive*. It's much better to use a knife-hand, a softer gesture when directing your captive ex-friend to a fighter that has probably claimed the lives of thousands of your system neighbours.

The hangar is large enough that towards the corners, where the air is space-stale and heavy, a miniature climate forms, and condensation drips down my neck, half-environment, half-exertion. One of the fighters is pried open by the wall, its entrails spilled across the metal floors. Around it, three boys in brown coveralls are struggling to replace the warheads and set up the changing station.

Shay knife-hands towards the fighter. "This one is yours. You can play with it as much as you'd like. Take it apart, put it back together, whatever, just make it shoot faster or something."

"Or *something*, he says."

"Or go faster, whatever. Make it into a better fighter so we can finish winning this thing."

Or whatever. I run my palm against the hull. It's smooth and shimmering and matches the temperature of the hangar impeccably. All fighters are finished with a UV- and Gamma-resistant coating for longer fights or transports.

If I close my eyes, I can still reconstruct the schematics of a fighter in my sleep, in any nightmare. This one is far newer than what I'd had the pleasure to fly, but the shape of it, the feel, is like stepping into my childhood home. Beneath the initial coating there are layers and layers of armour matrices interwoven with a network of intricate electronics. I walk along the hull, fingers gliding along the snakeskin-like coating. From touch alone, it's a good fighter. She'd handle beautifully with the right pilot.

"She's something, eh?" A reddish patch of hair pops from the cockpit. The boy is no less than a decade my junior and far too enthusiastic to be a pilot. Pilots usually have an air about them, a mix of superiority and martyrdom, like they're better than everyone else and aren't afraid to die to prove it. They are—better that is—but they also don't need to telegraph it so much. "Private Carte, Mechanic, First Class." The boy hops from the fighter and stretches out his hand towards mine.

"She still overheating after ten seconds of hard-burn?" I ask as I shake his hand.

Private Carte beams at me. "Ah, you've been around the Model 2s. We fixed it with a constant coolant wash. As long as the coolant is fresh, she can hard-burn as long as you want. Although that raised our coolant demands. Some solutions can create more problems, you know how it is."

I glance over at Shay who has wandered off and crouched against the wall. *Rest when you can.* He's picked up a few good habits since I've last seen him.

"And what's the charge like on her? 500?"

Carte laughs. "You know your stuff, but you're obviously from the last generation. The charge is in the thousands. It technically re-charges whenever it fires. Saves us time on resupply."

A lot has changed, and yet. "Then how are you losing?"

Carte pales. "Ma'am?"

"How are you losing to the breakaways when they have nearly decade-old schematics?" I glance over his shoulder and into Kaya's face, on yet another poster. This one has her features superimposed over her fighter, the *Iron Fox*. I wonder what the penalty is for setting one of these on fire.

"Ma'am, the Rule Eternal is not losing. We are winning a little more each day and will continue to win until the galaxy is again united and at peace."

Behind me, Shay stirs. "Leave the boy alone, Nez," he calls out. "You're just gonna upset him."

Carte freezes, mouth half-open. He's done his diligence in reciting the correct answer, the one any sane person would give in the presence of an Intelligence uniform. But I'm not here to throw around comforting platitudes.

Still, it *is* a good question. The Rule is technologically superior. They have pushed their fighter tech to its limit. The schematics that the breakaways have are nearly a decade old, and even if they worked on them and made their own improvements, they still shouldn't be able to compete with the Rule's manufacturing power. The sheer discrepancy in numbers should be enough. Maybe the breakaways just want it more. Then, before I can have a singular coherent thought, the hangar drops dead silent.

"The *Iron Fox* is back," someone bellows.

Shay leaps from his spot by the wall and grabs my arm. In a tone that's both warning and a plea, he whispers, "Let it go." The *Iron Fox*. My stomach churns. Shay squeezes my arm tighter. "Move along before you give yourself a stroke," he says.

But how can I let Kaya have her welcome parade without knowing I'm here? "I'll behave, just let me see her."

Shay doesn't buy a word I'm saying, but his fingers loosen their iron grip a smidgen.

"It's been more than ten years. I know the two of you are fucking. I'm over it. I'm not carrying a torch for her or anything, just let me see her."

Still unconvinced, Shay searches my face for any sign that I'm lying, telling the truth, anything in between. Meanwhile, the hangar erupts with deafening cheers and clapping. Dozens of pilots and technicians rush to the far end of the hangar where a fighter just pulled through decom—fighters are basically radioactive by the time they return. Measures need to be taken so that the techs don't get cancer every time they set one up for a re-charge.

Even from nearly fifty meters away, when the cockpit hatch slides open I recognize the flight suit-clad figure climbing out. Even with the opaque helmet and faceplate, it's unmistakably Kaya. There hasn't been a pilot, and arguably, never will be a pilot, who exits their fighter with such pizzazz. In a smooth motion, Kaya pulls the helmet from her face, and her long (very-much-not-up-to-code) hair spills down and past her shoulders in an obsidian waterfall. Even as a cadet, Kaya had the swagger of an ace. Even in simulation, Kaya performed as if it were her very last battle, leaving nothing on the field. Unless, of course, it was me.

Eyes blazing with a victorious high, Kaya surveys her adoring fans. "Twenty direct hits, fifteen kills, and two full-sized cruisers. Today we drink to the Rule Eternal!"

"Rule Eternal!" The crowd erupts louder still.

I manage to pry my arm away from Shay and stagger through the rear line of onlookers. I shove a few aside with my shoulder, ducking under pumping fists. Thanks to my dodging and weaving there's now only one line of enthused spectators between me and Kaya. By now she's climbed down from her fighter and is receiving good natured punches to the shoulder.

She's parked *Iron Fox* right above a copper spot on the floor, one that I imagine had been crimson not too many hours prior. Sacrifices have been long carried out by the fleet before major deployments. It's not uncommon for privates to volunteer their lives to assure safety of a Rule ace. If I ask anyone about it, they will all lie and insist that those are just rumours, but the floor begs to differ.

Then, Kaya sees me and her expression shatters.

She raises her right hand to silence the crowd as her face pales beneath the tan skin. In the ten years since I've seen her, *really* seen her, she hasn't aged a day. It feels right. Kaya is immortal in her beauty. In her zeal for victory she is as relentless and unyielding as the burn of a star. With every sacrifice carried out in her name, she is reminded of her importance. She motions for the row to part like she is a deity commanding the flow of water. If there was a chance to run, it's long gone now. Shay finally catches up, but he says nothing, and simply plants himself to my left.

"Nez?" Kaya's voice is small, child-like. She reaches out to me across what feels like a bottomless chasm.

In this instance, I could forgive, I could cast aside every unsavory bit that transpired between us, I could take her hand and move on.

"*Fuck you.*" I slap her hand away.

An unadulterated flash of pain twists her fine features. A hand from the crowd reaches for me, but Shay beats them to it and places himself inbetween. "Easy, no need for this to get messy."

Kaya takes a step closer so she's an arm-length away from me. The last thing I ever said to Kaya, I ever asked her, was to trust me. In a whirlwind of a tailspin, with the ground coming at us at neck-breaking speed, I asked her to trust me as a pilot, to trust that I would keep us safe. A deep ache, a not-so-gentle reminder, radiates from the base of my skull through my left arm, down my spine and through the leg. When everything was on the line, I wasn't willing to give up on us, regardless of the danger. Kaya was.

Her dark eyes trace along the jagged outlines of my body. The way my arm hangs limp in its makeshift sling. She finally looks me in the eye and winces. "I didn't know.

I didn't know it would be like this."

I could have sworn someone would have tackled me by now, hell, that Shay would have tackled me, but the crowd remains silent, and Shay dutifully remains by my side. "We could have both made it," I say, low enough, but the first row still hears me, and a slow rumble of whispers rushes through the hangar. "Do they know, your adoring fans? Did you tell them how you, as my co-pilot, decided to save your ass and leave me to die? Did you tell them how you never once saw me afterwards, never once called, never once apologized? And you had plenty of time. I was rotting away in that hospital for six months before they chucked me out. Did you tell them how I *begged* you—"

"Enough," Kaya cautions, but her voice is drowning beneath the murmurs from the crowd.

I'm too far gone to quit. "Did you tell them you professed your love to me not a week prior? How you whispered it in my bed? How—"

Kaya takes another step, her face an inch from mine now. She's nearly half a head taller than I am, so I tilt my face upwards to maintain eye contact. "I said, *enough*," she hisses.

"You saved yourself and left me a cripple." I make no attempt to keep my voice low. "I'll never fly again. I may as well not have a future at all. Look at me, look at *it*. It should be me on those posters, me in that fighter." I grab the front of her flight suit and yank her down to my level. "Good thing I've still got one good leg." With the final word, I slam my right knee into Kaya's gut as hard as I can without losing balance, controlling the distance. Kaya can't pull away. She wheezes and doubles over to the ground. Before Shay grabs hold of me, I manage another strike, and the pride of the Rule coughs and coughs as she curls up against the floor.

Blinding pain stabs through my brainstem and I collapse to the ground, not too far from Kaya. The stillness of the hangar shatters and now dozens of techs and pilots are pushing their way to the front, shoving one another out of the way, trying to get to their fallen idol. Shay, with that damn remote in his hand, shocks me again and this time I can't breathe for nearly a minute. When I can finally inhale again, Shay jumps on top of me and wrangles my arms behind my back.

"I told you to let it go," he growls. I usually have something witty to say, but in the pandemonium and the searing pain, I've got nothing. He's forcing both shoulders behind my back much farther than they can go. My left one is the first to scream out in agony.

"You're going to dislocate my shoulder," I shout against the ground, but amidst the noise, Shay doesn't hear, or chooses not to. The pain grows, radiates from the shoulder girdle through to the forearm.

"Shay!" I scream against the floor and my entire arm goes limp.

The scream is loud enough to get the closest crowd of people to stop. My arm is immobile, splayed on the floor to the side of me. Shay scrambles off my back and to his feet, stiffens up into a salute. Despite her gagging and coughing, Kaya does the same. Maybe this isn't about me at all.

A wave of hushed *Rule Eternal* ripples through the crowd.

The tip of an impeccably polished boot taps right by my nose, irate. The hangar around me has fallen dead silent. "How difficult can it be, Captain Lindin, to transport a single woman, with absolutely no money, nor social capital, nor combat abilities, when you have the entire Intelligence and Investigations at your disposal?" The voice, crystal clear, steeped in aristocratic diction, carries effortlessly towards the very last rows of people. It's eerily familiar.

"Ma'am." Shay is still frozen in his salute. "Ms. Kato was delivered as planned, with no incident. This, I assure you, is merely—"

"She struck my favourite, and may I add, most effective, pilot."

Where have I heard that voice before?

"Ma'am—" Shay doesn't get to finish.

Rough hands pull me to my feet. My arm throbs, hangs by my side as a pathetic, wet noodle. When I'm able to see straight again through the pain, the Third Daughter, *the* Ennis Rezál, the woman that graced the walls of my quarters when I was eighteen (and through my early twenties, don't judge me), regards the scene with lukewarm interest. The gold trim and buttons along her dark blue jacket flicker in the hangar lights. The Third Daughter's hair is nearly white, cropped barely high enough to never graze the collar of her uniform, but remains dangerously close to it. She looks me up and down, gaze never faltering. "Welcome," she says, "to my humble abode, Ms. Kato."

THREE

A T SOME POINT, *someone* split my lip. That someone (Shay) sits in front of me in the med-bay as an overzealous medical trainee botches my stitches. Shay wallows unapologetically, despite having no one to blame for his idiotic actions but himself. Naturally, the Third Daughter Ennis Rezál has removed him as my watchdog after his little display of incompetence in the hangar.

Then, before Shay had an opportunity to protest his demotion, Rezál reached for my arm. Her child-sized hands had a steel-like quality to them, cold and stiff. One clamped down around my wrist, while the other cradled my upper arm.

"This is going to hurt, Ms. Kato," she whispered, so close that the scent of her hair engulfed me. Honey, the expensive kind, one made by living insects. "Try to keep quiet." Her glacial eyes drilled into mine, with neither compassion, nor malice. Rezál was a shark, zoned in on her kill. Without further warning, she yanked my arm forward until the joint slid into its rightful place.

I did my best to stay silent, but a low moan forced its way past my lips (along with my soul).

"Hm." the Third Daughter cocked her head to the side with the same impersonal demeanor. Then, not a single word added, she turned her back to me and crossed the hangar. Waves of onlookers parted for her like the sea, their arms high against their temples in salute.

She moved with a rigid gait, her arms folded lightly behind her back, blues stretched across sharp shoulders. Before she was gone from view completely, she turned and tossed me one last glance, her eyes chilling despite the distance.

An hour passes. Still, the mere thought of the Third Daughter casts a cold wave over me. Shay, noticing my uncharacteristic silence, decides that it's time to stop moping. "We good?" he asks, without raising his face from his palms.

I try my lip and stretch it against the haphazard stitching. It will have to do. "If you let me pop your shoulder out, we're good."

"You're not strong enough."

"It's all angles." I hop off the table. The front of my unmarked blues is brown with drying blood. I give it a good sniff and wince.

"Ma'am." The young medic holds out a folded paper at me. "This came in through the tube for you." The tubes run across the entire ship, like blood vessels. Usually crew can just call one another, but on special occasions, a more formal means of communication are needed. The paper is sealed in wax. Archaic. Aristocratic. *Rich.* I pry the seal open.

I read the note over, once, twice, then turn to Shay. "I'm gonna need new clothes."

"No. You get one set issued. There are rules, Nez."

"The Third Daughter has invited me to dinner, *Captain* Lindin."

Shay curses and drags himself upright. The young medic stabs my left shoulder with something I don't care for, but the shoulder numbs, and it's the best feeling I've had in the last seventy-two hours.

BETWEEN THE CORRIDOR and Rezál's dining room, through the doorway, the very much *military* design of the ship gives way to classic décor reminiscent of First Earth aristocracy. Intricate appliqué peach wallpaper with white trim lines the walls. Four portraits hang in the hall, each adorned in matching golden frames. Mother Eternal, the matriarch of the Rule watches over her three Daughters with a cold and calculated gaze. Below, Ira Rezál, the First Daughter. Aera Rezál, the Second Daughter, and of course, Ennis Rezál, the Third Daughter, follow me no matter how I move along the room, matched in their icy glares. A long table runs through the middle of the space. I give a rap to test it out. It's an actual wooden table, I swear. It must have cost a small fortune to drag this far from any respectable planet.

"This way," hums a small woman dressed in a white uniform as she directs me to my seat. There are only two chairs. My sense of self-importance blossoms.

I circle the table's edge and take my seat before a spread of three plates, two glasses, and what has to be a dozen forks, knives, and spoons. The plates are bone china, rumoured to be all gone, unless of course, the last remaining pieces are in front of me. I'm so enthralled by the forks, and the knives, and the antiques that I fail to notice the door opening again. I'm still counting the utensils when I sense a presence to my left. Before I know it, one of the forks is in my hand and I strike, on instinct alone. In one smooth motion, The Third Daughter catches my wrist and twists it just ever slightly. My fingers unfurl and the utensil falls silently against the lush, burgundy carpet.

"Now, that's a dessert fork, Ms. Kato," Rezál says, her eyes alight with a playful twinkle. "You won't do any real damage with a dessert fork."

She drops my wrist, simultaneously grabbing one of the forks with her other hand and stabbing it into the table with such force that the teeth fully embed themselves into the wood. She rests her hand on my shoulder. "Now, *that* is effective."

"Except that now I can't eat with it," I manage to push out.

"Then ask the help for another," Rezál sings and waltzes away. She slips off her jacket and flings it far along the table. Her pearly hair, now pulled back, spills two strands on either side, framing her already razor-sharp face. She pops the top two buttons of a perfectly starched blouse open and pulls her own chair out with a rough motion.

I'm staring, and I refuse to apologize for it. Undistracted, I can study her. Every movement from her comes with great force, yet great accuracy, as she flows from one posture to another with military-like precision. It's uncanny.

She catches me staring. "You're oddly calm for someone in my company," she says, rocking back in her chair. "And in your position."

I can't help it, she's contagious. "And what position is that?"

"Dire, I'm afraid." She *has* to know what she's doing.

"I was informed it was *you* that needed help, ma'am."

"With what?"

"Winning a war."

Rezál tucks a strand of her hair behind her ear. "The war will be won with or without you, Ms. Kato."

"Then why drag me all the way here?"

"*Faster.* I need it done faster." Rezál unclasps her cufflinks and sets the golden pair on the table. She rolls up her sleeves, slowly, deliberately, never once looking away. "Six months. Can you end this idiotic war in six months?"

I flick the fork that's lodged in the table. It gives a low hum. "You want me to end a two-decade long uprising in six months?"

Rezál blinks slowly, seemingly bored.

When the Rule initially expanded, it did so rapidly, uncontrolled, a chemical reaction gone terribly awry. Many a-bloody annexations took place, the Rule quashing whatever resistance they encountered until new rebellions stopped forming. Sure, a few planets, and even systems, had to be liquidated to ensure this, but they achieved *stability*. They found *peace*.

The Rezáls established their matriarchal governance shortly thereafter.

Then hundreds of years of *peace* made the Rule lazy. Systems scattered along the edges began to ramp up production and stockpile arms, and the Rezáls dismissed it as local conflict. Then discontent hit a system far too proximal to the Rezáls for it to be an acceptable fallout of domestic squabbles. Hours later, a message reached the heads of the Rule that five systems were making a breakaway from the empire. The rest, well—

"Correct. I want you to win this war in six months, Ms. Kato." Ennis twirls her golden fruit fork between two elegant fingers. "I want you to list everything you'll need to achieve this and hand it in to me before you leave. You answer only to me and only I know your true purpose here. As far as anybody else will be concerned, you're here to optimize fighter maintenance. Understood?"

"And my punishment if I don't?"

Rezál scoffs in the most elegant way. "Why must you be so melodramatic, Ms. Kato? No punishment, no consequence." She pauses, waits for impact. I could thank her for the excuse to keep staring. "No legacy. I've been following you very closely for the past ten years, since your little *incident*.

Every bit of anarchism and anti-militarism you've spewed from your keyboard and into the ether has been to taunt me, to annoy me. Every single key stroke a deliberate attempt to land you in my company. Now you have me, you're telling me you're going to say *no*, and go back to your little shithole of an apartment to rot away the remainder of your days?"

The way she says *shithole* is breathtaking.

"I am your final chance at doing anything worthwhile with your life," the Third Daughter continues her onslaught. "I am your last chance to carve off a sliver of history for yourself. So, I will ask you for the second and the final time, will you end this war for me?"

How can I say no to that? How can I say no to the Third Daughter when her eyes are ablaze with fever and vengeance, and she's saying such wonderfully cruel things? "On one condition."

Rezál beams at me. "You are in no position to have conditions."

"And yet."

She only hums.

"When the work is completed and the war is over," I tell her, "sacrifice me to bless the victory. Christen your fighters my blood and leave me to rest."

Rezál smiles, all teeth. "Such melodrama, Ms. Kato, but we don't do that anymore."

"Pardon me, ma'am, but that's *bullshit*. I'm surprised your nails are as pristine as they are given the frequency that blood befalls them."

Rezál rolls her head from right to left, still humming to herself. With a smooth, calculated motion, now with a steak knife in her hand, she rises to her feet. "Sacrifice. Wasn't it once an engineer's greatest pride? To be absolutely certain that their last work would be their legacy that they are willing to die there and then. I didn't take you for a romantic." She closes the distance between us too fast for me to react. "Very well, Ms. Kato. Our contract is set, you will end this war for me, and *I*—" she grabs my right hand and drags the blade across the palm. The pain is sharp and sobering. Rezál's vice-like grip prevents me from recoiling. "Oh, don't be such a baby." The Third Daughter drops my hand and slices her own palm. Her gaze doesn't waver for a second. "And *I* will spill your blood to honour the new fighters, despite it being rather archaic. Have we reached an agreement?"

I nod, ever so slightly, torn between shock and awe.

She shakes my hand, her skin slick with both our blood. As our palms press against one another, time crawls to a stop, and I drown in Rezál's ice-like eyes. Her glare drills through me, pins me to the back of my chair like a butterfly to cork. Even her slender frame is imposing, towering over me as I'm confined to my chair.

For as long as I can remember, I have always been enthralled by beautiful people. How effortlessly and frivolously they cast others aside on a whim. Both friends and strangers become nothing but fodder for the cause. And how easily they are forgiven by everyone for the simple pleasure they bring to the eye, perhaps for the way their hair falls against their necks, or the sharp line of their jaw.

The Third Daughter is no exception.

And to think that in this moment of reprieve, she is her most gentle and mellow. As gentle as Rezáls get. It might be easy for some to be distracted by the white tablecloths and the pristine manners, but I never forget that it is the Third Daughter herself who orders entire planets vapourised, leaving refugees floating through the cold depths of space. It is the Third Daughter who ignores calls of surrender and eviscerated entire breakaway fleets. By her hand, millions have died. Unlike the two sisters who rose through the ranks by name alone, Ennis Rezál was the only to attend flight school, the only one to serve the frontlines.

The Third Daughter knows the taste of death, she knows the smell of danger, and she loves both. One rumour has it that, in her service years, she had a near seventy-five percent accuracy in a dogfight. Another boasted her to be the most decorated Rule pilot in history. Others claimed that the real Ennis Rezál perished in a crash and was replaced by a synthetic (more so than the original) replicant.

Far too many for all of them to be false.

"What a shame, I see it now, up close," Rezál mutters, eyes still fixed on me as if I am a snared rabbit. "If not for your unfortunate accident, you could have been quite beautiful."

I wait for the sting of her words to subside before I reply. "What a shame that time is linear, for you could have been born the First Daughter."

Rezál throws her head back and laughs loudly. Yet, her hand tightens around mine even as her crystalline voice spills across the room. "Then I'd already be dead, Ms. Kato."

I do my best to smile back ignoring the burning behind my eyes and across my palm. My thumb brushes against Rezál's knuckles, featherlight. "Yes, what a shame it is that time is linear."

FOUR

EZÁL GIVES ME everything I ask for, workspace, schematics, a coffee maker. She even concedes on leaving me unattended, as long as I report to her every other day with updates about my progress. Dinners, with the Third Daughter herself. I should be thrilled, but dislocated shoulder and brain electrocution aside, this has been far too simple. Rezál knows more than she lets on. There is no hiding from that gaze.

Nearly two hours later, I strip from my unmarked blues and step into a frigid shower.

If not for your unfortunate accident, you could have been quite beautiful. I slam my left fist into the shower wall. Once. Twice. It's a terrible grounding technique, but all the healthy ones take too much time. I have to swing all the way from my back, using momentum and gravity to make contact with the tile. My fist comes undone after the second strike. I don't have nearly enough muscle tone to the dozens of fibres in my hand to be effective, but the first two strikes do their job and a faint trickle of blood runs from the split skin.

Flashbacks of Shay's knee on my back, the scream of pain still fresh in memory. Impotence at the hands of Rezál, her cold fingers making easy work of my shoulder. There's mud where the seam of my trousers meets the edge of the socks. I'm not sure how it got there. The grey clay-like putty runs from my legs and down the draiI never wanted to be beautiful. I wanted to fly, to serve, to be of use to the Rule, to the Daughters. I wanted to be the best.

There's no hot water on ships, too much wasted energy to heat it, but even water warms up as it rushes through kilometers of pipe. The shower grows to lukewarm, and I press my forehead against the standard grey tile to steal a moment of rest. The pain grounds me, steadies my breathing.

You could have been quite beautiful. I could have been many things. I could have been Kaya, all smiles and adoring fans, climbing out of her fighter to deafening cheers. No, I could have been *better.* No pomp and circumstance. I could have done what she had and more, without sacrificing my dignity.

Quite beautiful.

It's no secret that the Rezáls are all genetically engineered. How else would Mother Eternal keep bearing only daughters to fight her wars? Yet, the Third Daughter is more than just a tally of good genes, she's a work of art. From her bone structure to the texture of her hair, and the timbre of her voice, whoever brewed the cocktail of DNA that created Ennis Rezál was more artist than doctor. *Everyone* knows it. She knows it. She's beautiful, like a looming storm, or flash of a supernova: deadly and impassionate.

Alright, then, if I'm not beautiful, what am I? At best, useful.

There are cameras everywhere. It wouldn't be long before Rezál sees my little outburst. I will have to work fast before she gets any unsavory ideas in her lovely, twisted head.

The tile is dangerously smooth under my feet. Before I manage to dry myself off, an officer is inside, sent on Rezál's orders. She has the decency to send a woman, or maybe, on the contrary, she knows far more about me than I let on.

"Did you have a slip, ma'am?" She looks up and down my wiry frame, doing a half-assed job of keeping her contempt concealed. I don't flinch. I let her eyes scan every last bit of my body, every last inch of my pasty flesh. It's a familiar look and I know how to bear it.

"Pass me a towel." I nod at the bench by the door.

She wrinkles a short, upturned nose. "Ma'am, I will call the doctor."

"You will pass me the towel." I take a single step towards her, the edge of her shoulder stiffens. "And you will get me a pair of coveralls. The ones that the techs wear."

"Ma'am, you have your blues. I can have an additional set requested." Stiff, impartial, just as good officers should be.

I wish for a bar of soap to chuck at her. "You're far too low on the chain of command to know who I am, but I assure you that while I might be a saboteur, an anarchist, or a terrorist, I am not a soldier, nor do I have any desire to be one. So, save me the experience of having to squeeze myself into a pair of blues again and get me a pair of coveralls." I take another step forward. The girl visibly recoils while her feet remain glued to the floor.

There are cameras here too. Rezál will witness this exchange whether she wants to or not. I want her to know that she can't push me around through her well-dressed pawns. If she wants me disciplined and obedient, she will have to break me herself. Surprisingly, this time the officer doesn't argue; there must be an earpiece on her for Rezál to give her direct orders. "Coveralls, ma'am." The officer heads out the door.

"Underwear too," I shout after her, my voice calling back to me in an echo.

I MAY HAVE grossly overestimated my abilities when I agreed to the terms of the Third Daughter's contract. A schematic flickers over me, white outline against a tall black ceiling. I lay in a small puddle of shower water from my hair, head resting in the crook of my right arm. Dread of upcoming failure aside, I'm quite comfortable.

Between when I pull on my coveralls and when I throw up the first holo-schematic in my workstation, I conclude that I *might* have missed several integral fighter upgrades in my ten years away. First, the cockpit is much smaller, since pilots fly solo these days. There's still space for a co-pilot, but it folds down on most schematics. I'm assuming it's only to be used in rare cases. Second, the charge on the plasma blasts is almost unlimited now, which means no one needs to be accurate anymore, only fast. I should check what the accuracy stats are these days for an average pilot.

Third, and this is most important. They upgraded the engine and now it doesn't overheat, well, unless, like the ginger tech told me earlier, you mess up your coolant. In sum, the Rule has effectively squeezed the tech to its last possible iteration, just as I had predicted. Granted, my prediction was nothing but speculation at the time. Now I know it for a fact, and I don't like it.

I shift my attention from the hologram towards the faint red glow of the camera peering through the dark. Hello, Third Daughter, I hope you're enjoying the show. Extending my right hand, I flicker through a series of blueprints with nothing but a bend of my index finger. Once. Twice. I stop at the detailed overlay of the cockpit. Enlarge the image with a twirl of the same finger. Yes, she'd be wise to keep a close eye on me.

The rest of the ship is nearing the end of its thirty-six-hour cycle; the rumble of boot-clad feet and the chatter of officers is dying down. Without any external stimuli, the body always settles to a thirty-six hour cycle. Someone went into a cave and proved it once and everything. Ease and efficiency, two factors that the Rule always keeps in mind, whether setting clocks on a warship or scheduling ammunition delivery to the front lines. I spend the next hour pondering if the Third Daughter sleeps at all, and if she does, whether she sleeps alone. And if she doesn't, sleep alone that is, would it be her favourite pilot in her bed tonight or an unsuspecting stranger? Who would dare visit the most cursed place in all the galaxy, surrounded by, I can only assume, hundreds of pillows and duvets.

You could have been quite beautiful.

No sense in moping. Schematics are only useful when you already have a good mental image of what the craft is. Like any good, creative saboteur, I know how to pull pieces of information together, how to scout out weaknesses and exploit them. But without taking apart a brand-new fighter, I can only absorb a good theoretical base of how these things operate, which would bring me exactly zero steps closer to winning a war. The only way forward is through a gutted fighter.

No time like the present.

No, rest when you can. I learned that the hard way.

I jerk awake to the discordant chants of *Morningstar! Morningstar!* The sweat pouring down my neck could have made me think I was waking up to a klaxon. My cot is pressed right against a wall shared with the hangar.

By the time my legs are in coveralls, the chanting falls away. The sound of a fighter launching at maximum speed nearly raptures my eardrums.

Who the fuck is launching in the middle of the sleep cycle?

There's only one pilot who has flown under the Morningstar name, and she is definitely not flying anymore. Unless—it takes less than a minute to finish shimmying into my coveralls and I'm off. The hangar is easy enough to enter now that there are dozens of techs and officers piling into it. I slip in with a group of especially rowdy pilots who reek of cheap booze and slur their profanities, stumbling on from the mess hall.

Someone gives my bad shoulder a jovial pat. "It's *you*."

That's never a greeting I want to hear. It's the ginger tech from before, this time with matching dark circles under his eyes. He's smiling like he's won the lottery but he's tired and at the end of his shift.

"What the hell is going on?"

"This way." He keeps hold of my shoulder and guides me along the far wall. The crowd is sparse along the way, and we can cover more ground as we talk. Normally, I have a strict "no touching" policy, but this is actually helpful. "They're playing catch and release," the tech says when we're far enough from the main crowd.

"Who are *they*?"

He stares at me like I'm a recruit who just asked about vacation pay. "The Third Daughter and Iron Fox."

Looks like Rezál is still flying. "What's catch and release?"

We find a secluded enough spot by the far wall of the hangar and make camp there. On the opposite end of the hangar, an enormous screen lowers towards the floor. The screen is split between a typical radar view and a live-camera stream from just outside the ship. I'm horrified to think about how much this all costs.

"It's a game. No shooting, just tag. The aim is to get your opponent in your crosshairs for five seconds. If they can't drop you in five, you get a point. Game goes up to three points."

Of course, they're playing a game in the middle of a war.

"It's good for morale," the ginger tech says, apologetically, as if reading my mind.

"And who usually wins?"

He shrugs. "Who do you think?"

The screen flickers and we're graced with a shot from the *Morningstar's* cockpit. Rezál's frigid glare is glued to her instruments. Only her face and shoulders make it onto the screen, but even such a narrow picture reveals the Third Daughter relaxed, in control. "Morningstar to Mother, Morningstar to Mother, please confirm flight path is clear for one-hundred klicks."

"This is Mother," the response echoes over the loudspeaker, "flight path is clear, you are safe to play."

Rezál smiles. The oxygen mask obstructs most of her face, but for an instant, her cheeks hover over its edge. "Mother, I'm just going to give our shields a little tap, please disregard."

"You're clear for a tap, Morningstar."

Morningstar takes a wide berth back towards the ship, its path glowing across the radar. In less than three seconds the live cameras detect its faint flicker. Within the next breath, the fighter is upon us, and the hangar erupts with a klaxon and drowns in red lights. No one moves. The klaxon dies as quickly as it starts. On the radar, the dot that is the *Morningstar* hovers deceptively still because the fighter is skimming right along the edge of the mothership, its burn triggering the shields. That's what the Third Daughter calls a tap.

"Ma'am, are we all done with the warmup?" Kaya's face pops on the screen, her dark eyes shimmering with the reflected light from the instruments. "Or do you need a few minutes?" Her voice has an edge to it, softened by the apparent humour.

"Oh, I think I'll be alright," Rezál chimes, "as long as you go easy on me."

Here, the Third Daughter is jovial, playful. She exudes the calm confidence of a pilot with pedigree. The vowels of her speech flow freely as she repositions the *Morningstar* again to face away from the ship. "Whenever you're ready, ma'am," Kaya says. "Catch me if you can."

Without a reply, *Morningstar* breaks away. Before Kaya is able to trigger her acceleration, there is less than three kilometers between them. By the time the *Iron Fox* starts moving, *Morningstar* flanks it and jettisons right past.

"*Fuck.*" Kaya veers to the right to avoid being taken up in the burn from *Morningstar's* engines. But she's no amateur. The *Iron Fox* rolls, still accelerating, and positions beside *Morningstar.* On the screens, Rezál's eyes dart ever so slightly to the right, where she's anticipating Kaya to be. The closeup of her face is detailed enough to see her skin crease along habitual lines as the *Morningstar* packs on the Gs.

Despite Kaya on her tail, Rezál remains calm. With a fluid, almost lazy motion she reaches above her head and flicks her thrusters to reverse. The panel ahead of her flashes red— Kaya has her locked in the crosshairs. The countdown is on.

"It's like you're not even trying, ma'am," Kaya taunts.

Rezál takes several quick breaths but doesn't exhale. She's stacking her breath. It all makes sense now. Kaya doesn't stand a chance.

"What's she doing?" mutters the ginger tech.

I dig my fingers into my left forearm from excitement. "She's winning."

When the time runs down to two seconds and Kaya has shrunk the distance between the two fighters to nearly four hundred meters, Rezál acts. She adds one final breath to her chest and hits her thrusters to full. In the first second, her fighter decelerates so much that Kaya no longer has a lock on it. In the next second the craft comes to a near stop as the *Iron Fox* barrels over it and into the black.

The deceleration is violent enough to throw Rezál forward against her instruments, but she retains consciousness and flips the thrusters back and accelerates. She's maxing out what an old Model 2 like *Morningstar* can do on a straightaway. Within a kilometer she has a lock on Kaya. The rest is history. Kaya veers left, then right, but Rezál has far more experience, far more stability at her disposal. The chase is over before it really begins, and the first point goes to the Third Daughter.

"I assure you, my dear, I am trying very hard," Rezál finally replies, laughter in her voice.

"Well done, ma'am. Ready for the next one?"

Rezál rolls her head around and chuckles. "Copy that."

"What is it that the Third Daughter brought you here for anyway?" asks the ginger tech, still standing uncomfortably close to me. The crowd's murmuring dies down, fixed on the screens.

"Optimising maintenance," I throw out without breaking away from the screens.

"Seems like a lot of trouble for optimisation."

"Ask her yourself if it bothers you so much."

They're off again. This time Kaya is careful. She keeps just far enough to maneuver quickly, but not close enough that Rezál can pull the same trick. This time their cat-and-mouse game is a lot more dynamic. The round will go down to their piloting ability and endurance.

Every few seconds, Rezál slows enough for Kaya to get a lock on her, only to roll unexpectedly and break the timer off. They're both sweating now, both pushing their piloting to its limit. When the timer ticks to four seconds and Rezál breaks the lock for what feels like the hundredths time, Kaya snaps.

"*Fuck*," she shouts loud enough that the people closest to the speakers wince.

"Language," Rezál taunts through her laughter. *Morningstar* deliberately races past *Iron Fox* close enough that

Kaya is forced to react to avoid collision. "Giving up so soon? Show some guts. Are you not the ace of the Rule's fleet?"

On the screen, Kaya's eyes narrow at the words. Her fighter jerks to intercept *Morningstar*, but Rezál is too fast. The muscles on Kaya's face tense as she grinds her teeth beneath her oxygen mask. "Fuck, fuck, fuck. Fuck this." Everyone in the hangar inhales in unison as Kaya's thumb grazes the small indentation on her controls and she fires on *Morningstar*.

A murmur scatters across the crowd.

The moment her thumb lifts, Kaya realizes she's made a grave error. "Ma'am!"

Rezál's eyes dart to her radar. She breaks formation and positions her fighter closer to the ship. *Morningstar* can outrun the torpedoes on a straightaway, but they're locked on and there's no way she can lose them now. "Morningstar to Mother. How are our shields looking?" Rezál keeps her eyes on the radar as the torpedoes close in. Calm. Only the glistening sweat along her forehead gives away her rising anxiety.

"Mother to Morningstar, shields are looking good. We are advising you to evacuate your craft immediately."

"No can do." Rezál arms her own torpedoes and continues her break-neck sprint towards the mothership. The hangar is deathly silent. "Can our shields take several direct torpedo hits?"

"Yes, ma'am."

"Roger that." Rezál looks directly into the camera. "I'm not happy about this, Kaya."

Kaya watches on, her eyes wide with terror. Rezál is no longer listening. The entire hangar is packed now. Seemingly every pilot and every officer is here, neglecting their sleep. They stand shoulder to shoulder in ominous silence.

Rezál stacks her breath again and drives her back and head into her seat. By my humble calculations she is far too close to decelerate safely. The flash of the *Morningstar* is clearly visible on the live camera. Yet, the Third Daughter shows no signs of slowing down. When she's only a kilometer away, she flips her thrusters and braces. As the thrusters fire a five-hundred meters, the burnout blinds the live camera. Then the hangar shakes with six close impacts and floods with both red and the cry of the klaxon. No one makes a sound.

"Multiple impacts," the ginger tech whispers. "Just sayin'."

"Stop saying it." I glance at the camera, still dead. The crowd breaks into a low murmur. The only animated feature on the screen is Kaya's face, still concealed with her oxygen mask. Her eyes are watering. If her anger and incompetence managed to kill the Third Daughter, it's all over for me, for everything.

Morningstar is nowhere on the radar. Rezál's camera broadcasts nothing but static.

Then, the overhead system crackles.

"*Morningstar* to Mother." Rezál's voice is thin, weak. She's panting between words. "Seems I fried my camera there for a second. Iron Fox, what say you we call this one a draw? I don't think I have another one of these in me today."

"Yes, ma'am." Kaya spits out and throws a salute, as if someone is actually there to see it.

"*Morningstar*, you are clear for landing if you wish."

Rezál gives a thumbs up.

When *Morningstar* pulls into the hangar alongside *Iron Fox*, the hangar erupts in cheers. I'm not surprised. To the spectators, Rezál has demonstrated why she is the Third Daughter and why she is in charge of all of them. She is superiority. She is grace. To Kaya she has demonstrated benevolence.

The cockpit flips open and Rezál pushes herself to her feet through the open hatch. The strain is there even through the compressive flight suit. When she pulls off her oxygen mask, her face is stained red. Blood runs from her nose all the way down the pointed chin and behind the flight suit collar. She gives a wary wave to the onlookers. "Go back to sleep. The theatrics are over." She staggers from the fighter on shaky legs.

Kaya jumps from her own fighter and runs to her, only to be met with Rezál's outstretched hand. But when Rezál is steady enough, she draws Kaya near and says something under her breath. Kaya gives her a nod, but it can't be a good thing since she slinks away quietly back to the *Iron Fox*.

"Go back to sleep," Rezál says again, firmly, and cuts through the crowd, dodging hands eager to drag her to the infirmary.

"She looks rough," the tech says. *Carte*. Carte says. I finally remember his damn name, now that my mind isn't clinging to the image of the Third Daughter on the spectacular brink of death.

"*Carte*, I'm sure she's done worse. Get some sleep." I pat him on the arm and disappear into the crowd.

By the time I reach Rezál, halfway through a desolate corridor, she's slumped against the wall with one outstretched hand. A thin strand of blood and saliva stretches from her parted lips to the floor. When she hears footsteps, she immediately wipes her face with the arm of her flight suit. Then she notices the uneven rhythm and realizes it's me. She visibly relaxes. With a crimson smirk, she throws her back against the wall and lets it take most of her weight. "Still got it," she mutters, and her teeth are stained red.

"You fired off your torpedoes to decelerate enough to maneuver. Clever. Still, couldn't have felt nice."

Rezál closes her eyes. "I think I cracked a rib."

"I think you did more than that."

Scarlet smears across her already perfect lips. Her hair is dyed with it, the ends clinging to her sharp jaw with perspiration. *Stunning*. Rezál's eyes stare blankly into the opposing wall as she traces the corners of her mouth with her tongue, tasting every bit of sweat and blood on her skin. In the private seconds she managed to carve out for herself, she's unclasped the top three bands of her flight suit. Her chest rises and falls as it strains against the remaining fabric. She's scared. Whatever happened during catch and release wasn't planned, and Rezál had to improvise. She didn't think she'd make it.

"That was good flying, ma'am," I say, and it comes out patronising no matter my intention.

Rezál rolls her eyes and pushes off the wall. Her legs wobble. Third Daughter is kept upright solely by her pride and experience. "That was fucking *excellent* flying," she throws over her shoulder and stumbles down the corridor.

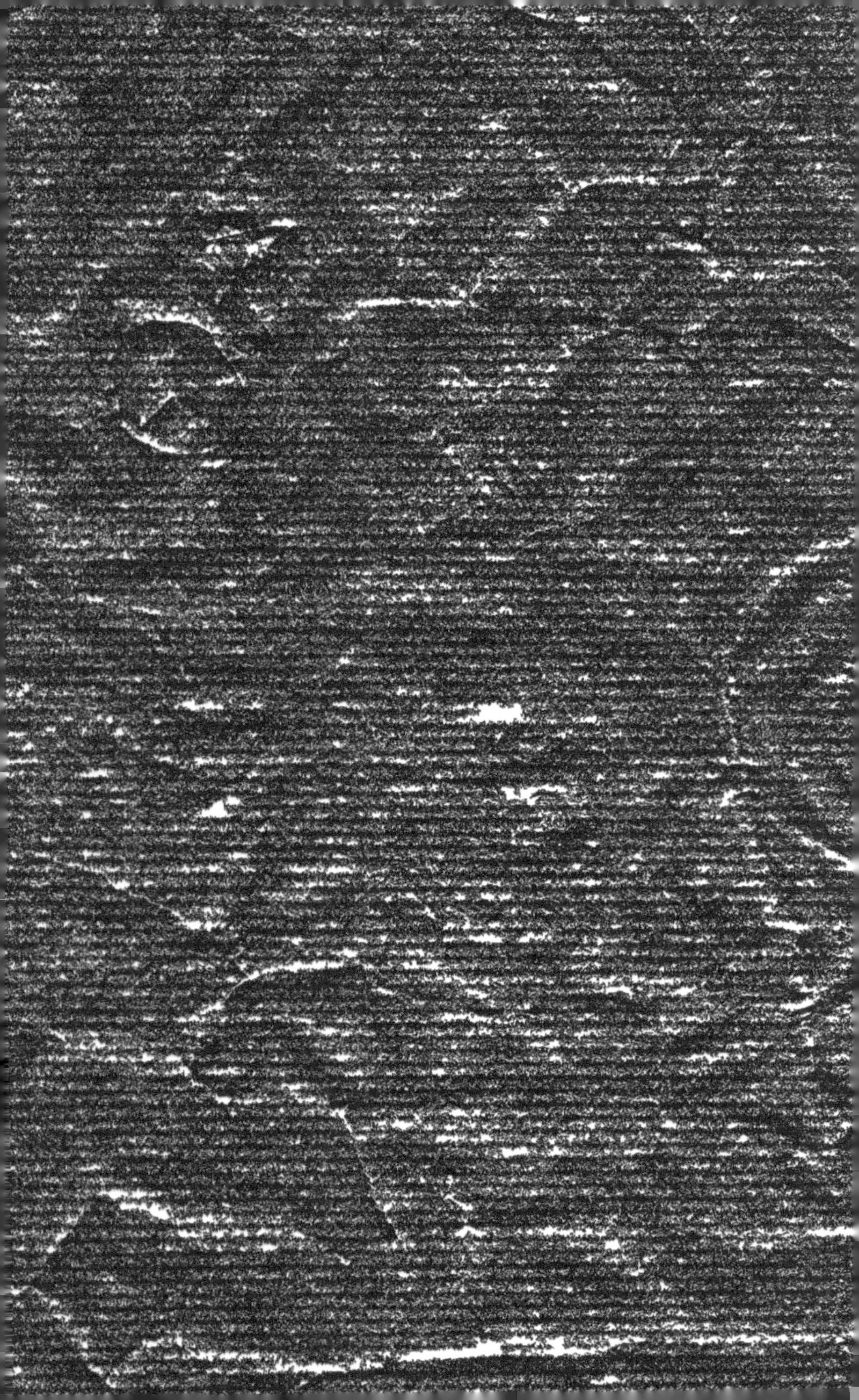

FIVE

MORNINGSTAR IS A Model 2 fighter.

The Third Daughter flies an outdated model with the speed and finesse of a brand new one. The victory, as I have always predicted, lies in the pilot, not the craft. When the thirty-six-hour cycle restarts I lay in my cot and listen to the clatter of magnetic soles on the other side of the wall. I'm not surprised to wake up with my hand between my legs, fingers slick from an exciting night I'm having trouble remembering. Whenever I close my eyes, the Third Daughter is there, taunting me with her blood-stained Cheshire grin. If she told me to strip in that corridor, I would have been naked before she finished the order.

You could have been quite beautiful.

Right. For the foreseeable future, my yearnings will be recused to the corners of my mind. I'm half-convinced that during basic training they primed us to find the Daughters irresistible, to instill morale, inspire devotion, make dying easier, the usual. Not that they needed to.

My generously assigned "room" is a home to a cot, a bedside table, and a single sink with a mirror. I make quick work of rinsing my hands and face, brushing my teeth, and strangling my hair into a semblance of a bun.

If pilots are the key to turning the tide, then my job is significantly harder. Harder, since pilots are not my expertise, nor my concern, professionally speaking. Harder still, since people are very difficult to *improve on*. People require training and psychological evals, and the right environments and stimuli to *get better* at anything. With my six-month deadline, I have no time for any of such improvements. It all comes down to the numbers. And if I want to fully grasp the state of the Rule's fleet, I need numbers from the best pilot that the fleet has—Kaya.

After last night, I expect Kaya to sulk for at least a full cycle. In our youth I would find her in the officers' bar, drunk out of her mind after an especially poor performance. Although, this time, I suspect she's gone to pay her apologies to the wounded party.

It's early enough that the hangar is nearly empty. The fighters are neatly lined, with two or three techs surveying the re-charging stations. It won't be difficult to sneak past them and on to *Iron Fox*.

"You're up early." Shay's voice catches me off-guard, since he is the very last person I anticipate running into in a hangar. We exchange curt nods. We're not okay yet, but strangely enough, we've been worse.

"Heard things got pretty rough last night," he says. That's one way to put it.

Does he know? Surely, him and Kaya are sharing a bunk, sharing a space intimately enough that he'd know about her comings and goings. *Surely*. I don't bother softening the blow. "How long has it been going on?"

Shay keeps to my pace, along the edge of the hangar. For every two steps I take he takes one. He silently raises an eyebrow.

"Kaya and the Third Daughter."

"What about them?"

She can't possibly be *that* good. "They're fucking, Shay."

For a moment, Shay falls behind. Like all air had been sucked from his body, he slumps forward, shoulders first, but catches himself with the next step. The skin along his forehead pales and a faint flush spreads across his cheeks. "No, they're not."

If only I were wrong, but I'm not. Kaya is ninety-nine percent bravado with the last percent reserved for honest vulnerability which she only shows those she's deeply in for. What I saw last night, the regret, the fear, were all real. I know how fear looks like on Kaya. I know her regret, intimately. I can't speak to Rezál's feelings, but Kaya is in deep, and Shay is a fool for not noticing it sooner.

"Where was she when you headed out this morning?" I ask Shay.

"Out."

I let him simmer in his answer. We walk the rest of the hangar in silence. Only when we reach the *Iron Fox* does Shay ask me what I want with Kaya's ship. "I want to see her stats," I tell him and start to climb towards the cockpit. "You're more than welcome to tag along, but it's gonna be boring."

Shay shrugs and follows right behind me. Despite the many upgrades, the inside looks exactly like any other cockpit. I can break my head trying to pull stats from the main computer, but it's much more useful to watch the recording from Kaya's helmet for any recent flights. It will tell me not only her firing stats, but also *how* she lands her targets.

"I think you misinterpreted something, Nez," Shay says, leaning on the bulkhead. He's far too tall to be in a fighter and has to scrunch his frame awkwardly to even make it through the opening.

Of course, he'll try bargaining. "Maybe," I tell him. "I have a shit read on Kaya's feelings anyway. Case and point." I gesture vaguely to all of him.

Shay winces. "Yeah, about that—"

"No harm done." I'm not about to discuss the intricacies of working with my ex, while one of my oldest friends is fucking her, while said ex is also shacking up with the Third Daughter. The entire fleet is one monstrous, incestuous wasps' nest, and I have no stomach for it.

I slip on Kaya's helmet. The padding is damp with last night's sweat, though the smell is not unpleasant. It's familiar and comforting in all the wrong ways. Curiosity gets the best of me, and I rewind the latest footage. Typical Kaya, she's swearing for most of it, trying to run Rezál down (unsuccessfully, *obviously*). Then, her voice drops to a hushed *oh no, oh no, oh no.*

Kaya: Ma'am, you have to abandon your fighter. You can't outrun the torpedoes for long.

Rezál: Do not tell me what I can and cannot do.

Kaya: Ma'am, I am so *so* sorry.

Rezál: You'll show me how sorry you are after we're done here.

They must have bypassed the broadcast, because this is the first time I'm hearing this particular angle of the conversation, and I have to say, I am impressed. Despite the acceleration, the Third Daughter is calm, collected, and *flirting?*

Kaya: Ma'am, this is a terrible idea, your fighter is old, you won't make it. Please, *please*, abandon your craft.

Rezál (voice straining against the G-forces): Kaya, my dear, watch closely, and *learn*. This, right here, is why Ms. Kato and I will always be better pilots than you.

I stop the recording.

"What?" Shay asks, his voice muted by the padding of the helmet. "What did you hear?"

"I don't know."

Why did Rezál drag me into this? What can she possibly know about me as a pilot to even justify such a thing? I was never in combat. Frankly, I botched the most important exercise of my career and ended up costing the fleet an abysmal sum of money. What can she possibly mean?

I rewind the recording farther back, all the way to the mission Kaya completed just as I was brought on. I watch as Kaya navigates the field, dodges, rolls, veers, does whatever is in her power to avoid getting killed. A slow disappointment rolls over me. "Shay, did you know Kaya is a terrible shot?"

"What?"

I'm almost surprised he's still here. "Her accuracy is like fifty-five percent."

"She has the highest kill count."

He's not wrong. "That's because she's fast."

The difference between Kaya and Rezál is that Kaya *reacts*. She does it quickly and accurately, but she doesn't anticipate. Rezál knows her field of flight well enough that she can anticipate how both her craft and her target will maneuver. That's why Rezál can outrun two torpedoes. That's why Rezál is a much better pilot. That's why the breakaways are winning.

If all Kaya is doing is reacting, then she is limited not only by her *reaction time* but also the time it takes for the signal to run from her pretty little eyes to her, what I only assume is a walnut suspended in fluid brain, back to her hands to fire. She can react as fast as she wants to, but there is still a significant delay. If I can shorten that delay, if I can make the pilots fly more like Rezál, I can win the war.

"Is that all you need?" Shay asks when I slip off the helmet. "What did you find out?"

"Not sure yet," I tell him and hop to my feet. "I need to talk to the Third Daughter and figure out if this is actually worth anything."

Shay nods and heads for the ladder. "Nez," he says, "don't tell me any more about Kaya."

I understand now. "I won't."

We don't talk much after that.

I AM UNDER no illusion that the reason I'm allowed this deep into the belly of the mothership, so close to Rezál's quarters, is because she is *letting* me. She is either too preoccupied to care about my whereabouts or she explicitly expects me to come to her with any news I have, even if it's outside our designated dinners.

But by the time I'm faced with the immaculately carved doors of Rezál's quarters, gone is all my ability to care. Do I knock? Is it appropriate to knock? Does the Third Daughter answer her own door?

I knock.

Kaya opens the doors with her hair tastefully draped over her naked breasts. Save for the hair, she is completely nude. At the first sight of me, her eyes widen, but she quickly regains her composure, and her swollen lips stretch in a self-assured smirk. "Nez."

I mirror her smirk, now that we both have something to be smug about. "Shay said I could find you here." Oh, what I wouldn't give to be a fly on the wall for *that* conversation later.

Kaya is stunning, luminous olive skin made only more beautiful with a perfect flush. The way she pouts with disappointment is tantalizing enough to make the most reserved swoon. Yet, even Kaya's beauty pales in comparison to Rezál's quiet, commanding presence. The Third Daughter is lounging on an antique armchair across the room wearing a bored look and an unbuttoned white dress shirt. She swings one leg over the other, and the blues of her uniform look more exquisite than any silk

I've ever had the pleasure of handling.

"Took you long enough, Ms. Kato," Rezál muses. She beckons Kaya back with a wave of her hand.

Third wheeling to the Third Daughter and my ex-girlfriend isn't exactly what I had in mind today. "I can come back later."

"Nonsense," Rezál purrs and parts Kaya's legs with her knee. "We can talk shop." She slides her hand down Kaya's abdomen, kissing her neck. When she reaches her goal, Kaya lets out a sweet little moan.

"Fine." I cannot stress enough just how much I do not want to be here. "Your favourite pilot is a terrible shot."

That dampens the mood. Kaya throws me a chilling glare, but Rezál seems unfazed. "How so?"

"She's sitting at barely fifty-five percent."

"That's not good." Rezál stops her ministrations. Before Kaya can protest, she asks, "Did you know this?"

"Yes, ma'am," Kaya responds wantonly.

Ugh. "Ma'am, she's the best pilot you have, I'm afraid that everyone else is probably averaging even lower. That's your problem, not your fighters. You need better pilots." Yes, let's make everyone in the room just as uncomfortable as I am. "You need pilots like yourself if you want to win this war."

With a drawn-out moan, Rezál pushes Kaya off her knee and gives her a hearty slap on the ass (no complaints there). "If Ms. Kato is right," the Third Daughter says, "you should be spending far more time in sim than here."

Let's make it worse. "Sims aren't going to help her, ma'am. She fundamentally flies different from you. She has a poor sense of her flight space and she's overly reactive. Unlike you, for example, who anticipates others' actions, Kaya simply shoots at whatever moves."

"I'm right fucking here, Nez," Kaya spits out as she collects her clothes.

"Her saving grace, ma'am, is that she's fast."

"Damn right," Kaya snaps, hopping on one foot to shove the other through a pantleg.

Still from her armchair, Rezál gestures at the door. "Kaya, *please*."

I expect a fight from Rezál's *favourite pilot*, but Kaya throws a stiff salute and, tits still out, shirt in hand, pushes past me into the corridor. She is still a good soldier. She knows how and when to follow orders.

As the door shuts, Rezál remains seated. There are no traces of last night's injuries on her. Nonetheless, a quick wince flickers across her otherwise perfect features. She takes a long breath, and in a strangled voice, asks, "Ms. Kato, if you will, on my bathroom counter there is a small glass vial. Bring it to me."

This could be interesting. "What's in the vial?" I expect her to lie or to order me.

"Something for the pain." She winces, this time for real, and her right hand forms a small fist. "I'd appreciate it if you hurried."

When I return, Rezál turns, visibly relieved. She takes the dainty glass container with a shaking hand and delivers two drops of the liquid into each, wide-open eye. "It's the most inconvenient thing," she says, throwing her head back against the headrest. "Last night took more out of me than I had planned. I'm not as spry as I once was."

"You're ill, ma'am?"

Rezál smiles. A tapestry of blue veins runs just beneath her pale skin, all across her neck, between her breasts, and through her eyelids. This up close, she's far too slender to be healthy. The tendons of her neck strain against the skin every time she moves. She takes a deep breath and sighs. "In a manner of speaking."

"It looks much worse than that." I'm not sure what to do with my hands, or where to stand, or sit, so I shove my left arm into my makeshift coverall sling.

"It is," Rezál whispers, nearly too quiet for my ears.

"You're dying." The verdict escapes me before I can stop it. An assumption such as this can cost me my head, a suggestion, that the Third Daughter may not be as strong as she appears. But the secrecy of it drives me forward to drag it into the light. Secrets. *Omissions.* They cause more trouble than they're worth.

"The Intelligence officer is being cucked, the best pilot is a terrible shot, and the Third Daughter is on her deathbed." Rezál snickers. "Ms. Kato knows all their secrets, yes, *all* the secrets. What shall she do, now that she knows the most destructive secret of all?"

She's still in pain, wincing with every word that spills from her lips. But there's a trace of emotion under the usual sharp tone, something primal that the Third Daughter has managed to bury up until this point. Then the pain grew too much, and it forced her hand, she was forced to act, to *ask*, to reveal herself to me. She's scared. Last night's fear makes far more sense now. No, the Third Daughter is not afraid of death. She is afraid of weakness, of fallibility. She's afraid of being found out. But her self-imposed solitude, necessary for the position she is in, is tightening around her beautiful neck.

I crouch down so she can glare at me without straining. "How is the pain?"

Rezál scrunches her nose, looks away.

"That's why you want this war to end in six months. That's how long you've got left, isn't it? You want to be remembered as the Daughter that managed to end the twenty-year war."

"I want to be remembered."

Don't we all? Isn't that the reason we all stayed with the fleet instead of deserting at first opportunity? Kaya, the ace, the stellar pilot. Shay, in Intelligence. Me—we joined because we didn't have a choice, we stayed because we wanted legacy. For three kids from Oran, a far-arm system, what other avenue did we have? What other opportunity would be granted to us, to make our names known to the people that mattered? We'd either turn our backs on our home or our future. We all made our choice.

There's no more time left for meandering. no more time left for strategic titration of information. The Third Daughter is ill and she may not see the end of this war if I don't act now. "What if there was a way to make your pilots better?"

Rezál raises a perfectly groomed eyebrow.

"It's a longshot. Something I've been mulling over for a while now. Just an idea for now."

The Third Daughter bares her teeth. "Well, do take your time, Ms. Kato. As we both know, I've got nothing but time at my disposal."

Even now she's capable of sarcasm. She's not quite finished yet. *Alright*, I can humour her. This long winded explanation has to start with a hook, something Rezál can latch onto, understand. "Ma'am, have you heard of dragonflies?"

Rezál props herself up on an elbow and leans forward, her eyes lit up with renewed vigor. "Dragonflies?"

"Nature's most efficient killer."

"A promising start, Ms. Kato."

I rise before her and extend my hand to the Third Daughter. She takes it without hesitation. When I pull Rezál to her feet, she wavers slightly and catches herself with her hand against my shoulder. Despite it being my bad one, I can easily bear her weight. Her eyes follow her arm to my shoulder and then downwards my body. She traces every contour, scrutinizes every feature, and finally looks me in the eye.

"No more formalities, no more secrets," she hisses through clenched teeth, and her breath is sweltering against my skin.

I'm right where I want to be.

"No more secrets, ma'am."

SIX

I LEARNED ABOUT dragonflies first as a child, amused by anything and everything that had the ability to defy gravity. Butterflies, dragonflies, paper planes. Dragonflies first came to Oran thousands and thousands of years prior aboard a colony ship heralding from First Earth, or so the fossils tell us. Far too efficient hunters for their own good, they soon decimated the ecosystem, nearly wiping out most of Oranian native insects. It took a few hundred years of self-regulation for the whole thing to fix itself.

As a gangly youth, I spent my summers buried to my ears in reeds, on a planet that is nothing but molten rock now, watching these aerial hunters do what it was they did best. I held on to those summers as best I could, but severe brain trauma tends to disregard treasured childhood memories.

Still, the remnants of a fractured memory had stuck, fueling my fascination with dragonflies well into adulthood, reignited once more by my desire for vengeful flight. I learned, at an embarrassingly late age, that the reason dragonflies are such efficient hunters is because of their uniquely wired brains and their highly efficient nervous systems. Unlike most other hunters, dragonfly brains can anticipate the position of their prey with frightening accuracy and attack nearly instantaneously. Their eyes also give them a nearly 360 degree view of the field. This is how Rezál flies. Instead of relying on visual cues, she holds the position of any fighter on the field in her mind's eye, simultaneously predicting where it will move to in the next second. Everyone else, including her favourite pilot, tend to track with their eyes and react, like the amateurs that they are.

"Then how are you proposing we fix this?" Rezál asks from her armchair. She retreats to it when her knees awkwardly give way and she nearly collapses on top of me. Now, she wears a familiar mask of indifference and takes small, staggered breaths when a new wave of pain washes over her.

I'm sitting on the floor in front of her, feeling like the most important person in the world. The Third Daughter can make anyone feel this important. It's all in the eyes. "We can't make them fly like you, but we can minimize the buffer time. Let's take Kaya for example. When Kaya sees her target, the signal needs to travel from her perfect little eyeballs to her hollow cavern of a brain—"

Rezan grins and doesn't say anything.

"—and then her brain needs to process it and send a signal to her fingers to fire. If we can speed this whole process up, give her a way to talk to the ship directly, we can probably cut down on a third of a second in reaction time. We can also feed camera and instrument readings directly to the pilots, so they don't waste time reading manually. If they start processing the ship positioning the way they process their own body's position in space, they'll genuinely fly as if the craft is an extension of their body, like you do. It's much easier to get them used to new inputs than it is to have them re-learn how to fly. It should be sufficient to improve everyone's averages. They wouldn't be nearly as effective as you are, but it could be enough to turn the tide on this war."

I'm not building anything revolutionary. I'm building a fancy translator for the pilots to talk to their ships and vice versa, without relying on their instruments. Super simple stuff.

"She was a mess when she got here," Rezál says, her gaze falling through me as the medication begins to take her, "after your accident."

"I'm sure."

"She didn't want to fly." She slurs a little. The rigid posture melts away and Rezál slouches low in the armchair, one leg draped over the other. "Kaya was too afraid after what happened. She was convinced she'd killed you."

"She did much worse than that." I absentmindedly pick at the nailbeds of my left hand, deep enough for the skin to peel. Limited sensation means that I can easily draw blood before I feel anything of substance. It's a nasty habit, one that I indulge in frequently.

"She did the right thing. *You* gave in to theatrics. She followed protocol. If she hadn't, there would have been two dead pilots on the ground and very much money wasted. Kaya did the right thing."

"I had it."

"You *didn't*." Rezál gives me a solemn look. "I looked through the records and you certainly did not *have it*. The fact that you survived at all was a miracle. You should be grateful."

Right. "She ended my flight career."

"And yet, you've done quite well for yourself, Ms. Kato."

"You're absolutely right, ma'am, I should be thanking Kaya on my knees for the honour of being kidnapped from my own apartment to try and salvage a losing war for the family responsible for blowing up my home system." Too far and too pointed. I'm speaking for too freely and the only reason Rezál is letting me is the sedation from her pain meds.

Slowly, with outmost effort, Rezál rises. Her arms tremble as she pushes off the armrests to stand tall, head high and unyielding. The pain medication has diluted her irises large enough that they nearly flood her eyes black. "Take it from me," she says, "these things are never fair. You'll drive yourself mad thinking of how it could be different." She staggers past me into the bathroom. For an anguished second there's silence and then a thud.

I find the Third Daughter on her knees before the toilet, the ends of her bleached hair clasped in a small fist behind her neck. She retches softly and slumps back against the tiled wall. "Your guess is not enough. Pull the data from the rest of the fighters and tabulate the averages. Recruit a few techs for this if you want. Then, figure out a concrete way to shorten the time between—" Rezál throws herself towards the toilet again and empties the remaining contents of her stomach. She doesn't bother turning to face me. This time there is a smear of blood on the back of her hand. "—shorten the time between reaction and firing. *Go*. And I won't need to remind you to keep your private observations private."

"Ma'am—"

"Do your fucking job, Kato, or I will melt your brain, so help me Mother Eternal."

Usually, I'd take an order like that and run with it, but there's something endearingly pathetic about Rezál in this moment. The Third Daughter is in agony, on her knees, vomiting into a toilet like an overzealous recruit who had too much fun on leave. This is surrender, and if I'm to ignore it, I'd be just as bad as Rezál.

Despite every fibre of my body calling out against it, I take a bleached hand towel from the rack and wet it in the sink. Then, I get down on my knees beside Rezál. She's far too weak and doped up to protest when I wipe the blood and bile from her lips and her chin. "Does Kaya know?"

She silently shakes her head.

"Anyone at all?"

"Why? So, they can dump my memories into the next iteration, like they did with Aera?" She rests her forehead against the porcelain.

I don't have anything to add. I just continue to clean Rezál's face best I can until she closes her eyes and drifts off into a shallow sleep. After the schematics were leaked, Aera Rezál, the Second Daughter, was supposedly so ashamed of her failure that she took her own life. At the time, the Third Daughter was only rising through the ranks. It took all of two weeks to strip Aera's brain of anything worth of value and to shove it into *the next iteration*. Ennis became aware of everything she needed to assume command. I'm not certain the Rezáls know which memories are theirs and which belong to their sisters, where the legacy ends and they begin.

We sit together on the bathroom floor until my ass goes numb and I lose track of time. Eventually, Rezál slumps against me without waking up. I don't bother moving her.

In her sleep, the Third Daughter looks much younger than I ever imagined. She is far too young to bear the responsibility that is upon her. She is far too young to spread death as casually as she does, and yet—I brush a strand of her hair away, slick with sweat and bile. She'll fight until her dying breath, I know this. Now, with sterile tile beneath us as we catch this moment's reprieve, I understand what Rezál told Kaya last night. *This, right here, is why Ms. Kato and I will always be better pilots than you.*

Rezál and I are willing to die for what we believe in, no matter how twisted our idols.

SEVEN

LYING FLAT AGAINST the cold floor of the mothership, I scroll through the thousands of datapoints I've pulled from all the fighters. Like the good little problem solver that I am, I follow Rezál's orders and tally all the shot ratios for every single pilot (which is a lot), on every single ship (at least fifteen in this quadrant). After three days of polite coercion, the other ships graciously dump their ratios into my storage this morning and promptly crash the system. Three hours later, I have the system up and running again, and I'm beginning to make sense of this ocean of data. If the Rule really wanted to become the most efficient version of themselves, I should have started with their operating systems. They're *old* and *clunky*.

If I lay on my left arm long enough at this angle, it will slowly dislocate from the shoulder girdle, and I will land myself in medical again. I sit up and tuck the arm into my coveralls. The nagging throb slowly dissipates.

"Are you making progress?"

Rezál's voice is booming against the general hum of the ship, and I scurry to my feet to face her. My left side seizes up and my arm spasms along the bicep and forearm. I let out a small yelp and cradle my hand and forearm with my other hand. It will be another ten minutes before the ache goes away.

The Third Daughter regards the projection, impassive. Any signs of her illness are gone. Her hair, no longer bloody nor slick with her sweat, sits neatly above the immaculate high collar of her blues. With crisp posture and a slight frown, she injects herself into my workspace. "Ouch," she hums. Any reciprocation of the exchange we shared the other night clearly isn't happening.

"The ratios are awful, ma'am."

Rezál waltzes past me to get closer. "These don't look tallied up."

I grate my teeth. "At first glance, the ratios are awful."

"But you aren't certain." She's in a *mood* today and I suppose it's up to me to figure out which one exactly.

With a wave from my right hand, the projection warps. The numbers rearrange in neat columns with several digits highlighted. "There," I say, scroll the columns all the way down, and flick a highlight over the bottom row. "Now, I *am* certain that your ratios are awful."

Did I have the instructions pre-written and queued up only for Rezál to show up so I could do the math right in front of her? Maybe. All this just to impress the Third Daughter? Definitely. It works. The room temperature rises by a degree.

"Most of your pilots are sitting in the forty range. Which isn't *that* bad, but when compared to—" the projection disappears, and I pull another one from reserve. This one has fewer data points but slightly higher averages. "—compared to the breakaway averages. They're sitting at nearly fifty-seven percent. This is a tabulation of *hit* ratios from the other ships, not every hit results in a dead fighter, but I thought you'd want to see anyway." I highlight the bottom row again and watch Rezál try to make sense of the numbers. Her narrow nose scrunches as a small grin tugs at the corners of her lips. I'm not sure if she's actually impressed, but she does seem entertained.

"And finally—" with a flick of my wrist the projection shimmers and turns into a graph, trending downwards. "These are Kaya's averages over the past few years. The red line are her kills. The yellow is her average speed per flight."

Rezál scoffs. "She's getting faster *and* sloppier."

"She's adapting to the tech, but not improving her skill," I conclude and fold up the projection. For a few moments, Rezál keeps her eyes poised at the ceiling. Then, she runs her index finger just underneath her nose and comes back bloody. Gracelessly, she wipes the blood on her trousers.

"Ma'am—"

"No formalities, no secrets," she hisses. Her top lip is stained red.

"You're at a stalemate. You have the tech and numbers, but they have better ratios. You can draw this out, yes, and win eventually, but not in six months."

With the cadence of a stalking predator, Rezál approaches, so close that our shoulders graze against one another. She keeps her voice low, flat. "Ms. Kato, you do quite well at skipping the formalities, and yet you've failed to reveal your secrets to me." In the next moment, her hand is around my bicep, squeezing hard enough to bruise the flesh. "But you forget that you are not a guest here. You are here because I *summoned* you. You are unharmed because I *wish* it. And if you don't start talking, right now, I will change my mind."

"Ma'am—"

She shushes me. Her fingers tighten around my arm enough that it hurts. "Did you think I'd be stupid and not check your personal storage? Your computer drives? Did you think me so naïve that I would simply let you prance around my ship unattended? I've given you far too many opportunities to speak the truth." Rezál leans over until her lips brush against my ear. "Now, I'm going to *make* you talk."

She hoods me herself, then stabs with a sedative. *Rude.*

POPULAR MEDIA WILL have you believe that the Rule will pull your fingernails off and break your toes to get you to talk, but physical torture is messy and ineffective. That's not to say that Rezál won't resort to it, but if she does, it will be more for her personal enjoyment than results. When the hood does come off, I find myself in an aluminum grey room, no larger than a cubicle. I suppose the space could be easily hosed down for a cleaning without removing any of the furniture. I can appreciate the no-frills utility.

I clank my heels together—magnetic. I'm still on a ship. It's safe to assume that Rezál wouldn't waste valuable time by moving me. Someone has hastily tied my arms to the armrests of my chair with zip ties. The one on my left is too tight and my fingers have gone numb, which is only marginally more distressing than the usual lack of sensation. There are at least three cameras. Two by the ceiling and one in the wall to my left. The fourth camera walks in pinned to Shay's jacket.

"You're the idiot that tied my hands," I slur at him, and a glob of saliva slides down my chin. Sedatives take a while to metabolize.

Shay avoids my eyes, his eyes tracing the contours of my face, never landing anywhere specific. His whole face is flat of expression, pupils slightly dilated. Intelligence cares about the wellbeing of its officers and interrogators, even the chemical kind of torture can be draining. It's not uncommon for them to use mild sedatives on themselves to lessen the strain. If it does come to roughing me up, whatever cocktail now surges through Shay's bloodstream will make sure he doesn't lose any sleep to nightmares.

Rezál is deliberately messing with my head. Hence the zip ties, hence Shay. Then again, he'd agree to participate even without chemical assistance, he's a good soldier. But the Third Daughter wants him effective. She's watching. "You're gonna have him slap me around now?" I shout, hoarse. "We've watched the same orientation video—physical torture produces sub-par results."

Shay reaches down to the zip tie around my right wrist and roughly tugs it. This tightens it hard enough to stop all blood flow to my hand. *Well, that's not good.*

"After two hours you'll begin experiencing muscle damage," he says, low. "After four you will probably lose your hand. Although it may be less than four. We should probably start talking now so we don't waste any time. You don't have much." He draws back and leans against the wall. "Is there anything you want to tell me, Nez?"

"You're a sociopath and a fucking sellout."

Shay scoffs. "Fine. I'm going to have my lunch. I'll be back in an hour. Hopefully your attitude changes by then."

"You're just pissed because you're getting cucked!" I shout at the closed door. Even with Shay gone I'm not alone. No, the Third Daughter is always watching and she's enjoying the show.

WHEN YOU CUT off circulation, first the limb goes pleasantly numb, then it aches, then the pain climbs until you're willing to chew off your own hand to make it stop. By the end of the hour, I'm just about ready to start chewing. Unfortunately, I can't reach the zip tie with my teeth, nor can I snap it no matter how hard I strain. *Sucks to be me.* With every additional yank, the zip tie digs deeper into my wrist. I split my skin twenty minutes ago and now I'm bleeding all over the armrests.

Yelling at Rezál proves useless, no matter how satisfying. My only chance is for Shay to return and question me. *Fuck.* The fingers on my right hand stopped responding ten minutes ago. I need them. My left side is so impaired that if my right goes, I'll have no way to work, no way to go about the world. No way to—*fuck. Fuck. Fuck.* Panicking doesn't help. *Think. Think.* Let's try a different tactic.

"Ma'am, if I lose my right hand I won't be of much use," I shout. "I know you want me for my brain, but I need a way to work the projections." The door opens. I half-expect to see the Third Daughter in the doorway, but it's only Shay. He has mustard on his chin and if I wasn't tied to a *fucking chair,* I'd kick him in the gut. "How was your lunch?"

Shay doesn't respond. He shuts the door and takes, what I can only assume, his interrogation stance. "Are you ready to talk, Nez?"

"Once you untie me."

"That's not how this works." He throws a glance at one of the cameras by the ceiling, seeking approval. Shay always needs approval, it's probably how he got himself doing this job. "We cracked your personal storage, Nez."

Great, Rezál got impatient. She has another couple of hours to play with me, but she's really pushing. She's not used to running into closed doors and it's souring her mood. "I'm on the edge of my seat, Shay."

"What's on your drive, Nez?"

Shay's just a mouthpiece here. I do my best to ignore the pain and look up at the camera. "You got into my storage, and you can't make sense of anything because I'm not an idiot and I encrypt everything. You're paranoid or desperate, or—"

A speaker crackles. Rezál's voice comes from behind me. "Cut her arm off, Captain Lindin."

"Which one, ma'am?"

He seriously needs clarification?

"I couldn't care less." Rezál is pissed. But there's something else in her voice—wariness? Maybe it's the speaker, but the Third Daughter's voice is hollow, choked up, like she's trying hard not to throw up. She's getting worse, but not nearly as bad as I'll have it in a few seconds.

Shay hovers over me with an unsheathed heat knife. That blade will cut through actual starship hull. It's a bit overkill on my bony little wrists. I strain against the zip tie again and this time the plastic severs something important because the blood seeping from the cut turns from bright red to burgundy. "Shay, I swear to Mother Eternal, I will end you. I will find you and I will end you if you so much as touch me with that thing. I will destroy everything you love, Shay. I will—" I'm rambling, I *know*. I didn't anticipate him to actually do it. I didn't factor in just how devoted Shay is to the Third Daughter. I miscalculated, *badly*. Shay lowers the blade to my wrist. *Fuck. Fuck. Fuck.*

"Shay, don't you dare," I hiss. "I will tell Kaya, I will tell your mom if I ever make it out of here alive. I will—" I scream when the edge of the blade singes the hairs on my forearm. "Fine!"

Shay pulls back at once.

"Fine, you win. The encrypted data, it's a prototype. It's schematics for an implant that will get your pilots to interface directly with the aircraft." Amidst everything, I start crying. Disgusting, ugly crying. But I have to keep talking or Shay will start with the heat knife again. "But it's a prototype, I'm not even sure if it will work. It's not a viable product."

The speaker crackles behind me. "You will decode it then, and I'll judge the rest for myself."

"Yes, fine, whatever you want. I'll decode it. But it's not ready."

Rezál sighs on the other end of the line. "Captain Lindin, you've done enough, you're dismissed."

Without an acknowledgement, Shay sheaths the knife and leaves. I'm certain we'll have plenty of conversations about what just went on in this room. Notably, he does not cut me loose. This, I take personally.

Still zip tied, my face smeared with snot and tears, I look up at the Third Daughter. She's taken Shay's place, slipped into the room like a ghost. With the same lukewarm expression reserved for watching a pot boil over, she pulls out a handkerchief and wipes my face clean. She crouches in front of me and grabs hold of my chin, her eyes drilling into mine. "Now, Ms. Kato, you place me in a difficult position. On one hand, your work may prove quite useful to me, on the other, this is far too convenient for my tastes. You understand, of course. You're not an idiot." She throws my face aside and drops the handkerchief in my lap. Her slender fingers trail along the angry wound on my wrist, waiting for me to flinch. I don't give her the satisfaction, even when she scratches her fingernail right along the cut. "Why, oh why, would a failed pilot spend all her time devising such a piece of technology if she wasn't set on using it to ruin me?"

"I'm not a failed pilot," I push out through clenched teeth. Rezál's nail is still tracing along the wound. I swear she's increased the pressure. "I did not fail. I got fucked up. I got discarded. You said it yourself, I am a better pilot than *Kaya*."

"You could have been."

"I still can be." I force myself to meet Rezál's grey eyes. If she wants to hear it, I'll give it to her. I can spill my guts on command. I was a soldier once. "I can't make this implant myself, but you can. You have the resources, the staff, the materials. You can turn every pilot you already have into Kaya, better even. You can even get me flying again."

Rezál searches my face for a tell, and when she finds none, she breaks out in loud laughter. "All this so you can fly, Ms. Kato? All *this*?" As she laughs, the edge of her shoulders softens, and her eyes regain their murderous twinkle. She pats me on the knee, twice. "Get cleaned up and get to work. I expect the decoding done by the time I wake up from a much-needed nap."

"Ma'am," I say, with a voice that is embarrassingly small, "even with your resources you can't skip stages in development; the implant is a prototype. It needs to go through several rounds of adjustments, maybe animal trials, with rats or something, before we even consider putting it into a human pilot."

With a flick of her wrist, Rezál cuts the zip ties with a small pocketknife. "Then, Ms. Kato, to satisfy your yearning for flight, you will be my rat."

Rusted water runs from my arms, down my body, and into the drain. Every inch of skin stings, not enough to really hurt, but enough for the sensation to populate my mind until it's the only thing. Rezál has assigned the officer from the first day to supervise me as I shower, half to remind me that her eyes are always on me, half to make sure I don't kill myself. I wouldn't, but I shouldn't dwell too much on finding an opportunity. The fingers of my right hand are still sluggish, but the feeling returns, and with it renewed pain. In my struggle I also managed to subluxate my left shoulder. Fortunately, the arm fixes itself as I undress, but not without a blinding jab of pain.

It's the little things that wear you down, that strip away your last bits of self-respect. It's your friend, void of expression like the deepest corners of space, administering hurt in ways meant just for you. It's your old lover in someone else's embrace. It's the reality that even when I bait Rezál, I do it in her language. When I throw jabs at Shay, at Kaya, I do it in the language of the Rule. And the alternative? A stale and dark apartment, solitude, an aimlessness of my days, that makes *this* the better option.

Because this is still better than receding into obsolescence. *This* makes me the focal point, of violence, of torture, yes, but a focal point nonetheless.

I press my forehead against the tile and allow myself to *feel*. Feelings hinder. I've learned to turn them off a long time ago. Feelings keep me from being effective, from proving myself. These parts need to stay turned off until the right opportunity, if one ever arrives. A mixture of nausea and panic hit me. The sight of my split-open wrists is enough to send me to the floor, sobbing again. It's only been a couple of hours and the damage is still fresh.

The dread washes over me.

Of course, it would be *me*. Rezál would never volunteer her favourite pilot to be cut open like an animal, to be tested on, to be subjected to such cruel uncertainty. And I would never volunteer anyone else. It's *my* prototype. It's *my* work. It has to be me.

And that's exactly what I hoped for from the beginning.

My face hides behind my wet hair so the officer doesn't see me smile.

What? Did you think I was telling the truth this whole time?

EIGHT

LET'S BEGIN UP in the stratosphere of Edex, midway through a war game, when I realize both that I'm losing control of the fighter and that my suit has a leak. For a moment, I think that Kaya will actually listen to me and stay. The leak means that if she ejects, it will depressurize completely. When that happens, the blood in my veins will boil, and I will likely die. I ask Kaya, *beg her*, to trust that I can land us safely, but I can see that her decision has already crystallized. She doesn't apologize. She pulls the cord and in an instant, she is gone, safe, while my blood boils, just as I predicted. This is the last I see of Kaya in person, her fear etched in my memory forever. The next time I wake up, I'm immobile and mute. All I can feel is a scorching agony spread across the left side of my body, and then darkness welcomes me.

I begin to plan the downfall of the Rule sometime between when Kaya ejects and when I can form my first coherent thought, three months into therapy when the destruction of Oran gets picked up by every media platform. The next year blurs together, half from the painkillers, the other from the grueling impotence of being able to do absolutely nothing. But my efforts are rewarded when the news of the Third Daughter's fighter crash reach me.

Being the only Daughter to actively engage in combat, Ennis Rezál emerges with her dignity intact, even after losing an especially glorious dogfight near the frontlines. That's all the information that's released. It's bad. If it wasn't bad, Mother and the rest of the Rule would be parading her on every media platform not hours after the fact.

With the Third Daughter badly injured, or (fingers crossed) dead, that leaves only the Second Daughter, Aera Rezál standing at the helm of the Rule fleet. Aera Rezál has always had an impulse control problem of sorts. A few years back she vaporized an entire system because it was taking too long to surrender. Which makes me think that if I were to manufacture a crisis, Aera would respond in the worst way possible.

As therapy progresses, I realize that, while my short-term memory is in shambles, my memory of the fighter schematics is completely intact. It doesn't take long to recreate them and *leak* them to the breakaways. The harder task is to leak the schematics in such a way that they would be intercepted and brought to the attention of the Second Daughter. Surely enough, if I relay them through the closest ship in orbit, they will get flagged by the computer. Bounce the message off enough ships and you create mild military unrest. Everyone starts pointing fingers. People get tossed out airlocks. Petty stuff.

But Aera hears about it.

In true Second Daughter fashion, the news shatters her confidence and she overreacts in the most glorious way and promptly kills herself (honestly, probably by accident). Truthfully, I thought she would gracefully step down as

Fleet Commander to spare herself the scandal, but the Rezáls don't half-ass anything.

But then the unthinkable happens.

Prim, pressed, and completely upright, the Third Daughter appears on every media channel to declare that she will be assuming the role of Fleet Commander as replacement for the Second Daughter. It's been at most a month after her crash. A month after *my* crash I was eating most of my meals through a straw and pissing into a leg bag. It doesn't make sense.

Sure, the Third Daughter has access to every therapy under the suns and dozens of elite medical professionals at her beck and call, but *come on!* It's been a month. She's not superhuman (and not a synth, probably). I have no other choice but to start digging and I start with the Third Daughter's therapy team.

Because everyone falls in love with their therapist. They're trained to be compassionate, to hold your body in ways that are comforting and not at all painful. There's something utterly disarming about another person witnessing you re-learn to swallow and piss, and still treat you like a person. I bet my good arm that the Third Daughter has fucked someone on her therapy team. It's *Rezál* and a mere mortal therapist. Whoever it is, they stand no chance, even if she is in literal shambles. It's easy enough to figure out which schmuck she's bedded, and this gives me blackmail. Not for Rezál, no, but for the therapist. No therapist would stay alive if they were to start broadcasting that they fucked the Third Daughter, and I can make it appear so. Thus, after a little back and forth, I have complete details of Rezál's crash and her prognosis, and the therapist has peace of mind.

Next, I need Rezál to notice me. Currently, there are about three thousand degrees of separation between me and the Third Daughter, and I desperately need to narrow them. During the next few years, the fighting in Rezál's quadrant is constant and I work hard to remain the *thing*

on her mind. I leak some strategies to the breakaways.
I triangulate these communications through Rezál's
own networks so that she is always on guard, always
suspecting. I titrate this information. Come at her at
random intervals, unrelenting. As her health begins to
slowly decline, she grows more paranoid, and by the time
she finally summons me, she's ready to burn the whole
galaxy down just to secure a victory.

Kaya's presence on the mothership is an unpleasant
surprise and I'm forced to improvise. I don't feel any
particular way about Kaya, but the Third Daughter needs
to believe that I am acting independently. I can't have
Kaya nor Shay getting caught in the crossfire of what I'm
about to do. But "the disabled pilot who wants to exact
revenge over the ex-lover" is an easy sell and after our
little brawl in the hangar, I think Rezál buys it. For the
record, I didn't know they were fucking. It was a surprise
and not of the pleasant variety. Maybe I do feel about
Kaya some sort of way, or Rezál. Anyway, I don't have
time to unpack it.

Now, getting the Third Daughter to rally behind my
prototype idea is a little harder. Rezál is smart and has a
good nose for bullshit, which means if I bring her the idea
myself, she'll smell sabotage and probably throw me out
an airlock. Instead, I make her claw the prototype data
out of my proverbial cold, dead hands. When we have to
work harder for an outcome we tend to believe that it's
more worthwhile. It's a strange tendency, but one that has
held true for me so far.

Even though Shay lets me destroy one of my computers,
I know that the Third Daughter will dig through all of my
personals. She's not too trusting, which works in my favour.
I just happen to leave the prototype schematics lying around
so that whoever is raking through my data can find them.
But even that would be too convenient for the brilliant
Third Daughter, I have to admit, it *is* too convenient for me

to have these schematics. I need to give her a reason for their development, a good reason, an emotional reason. From the time I set my foot on the mothership, I convince Rezál that my "incident" has left me shaken, bitter, unfulfilled. I telegraph my disdain for Kaya, the ace pilot. I put on a jealous face, jealous of beauty, of success, of ableness. By the time I cry to Rezál that the implant would help me fly again, she's ready to believe it. Why wouldn't she? She's done the same. She's mutilated her body to assume command. Sacrifice runs in her veins.

This is my opener, and I've played it to perfection. The rest, is well—*Oh!* I have to die because I *really* don't want to be around for when Rezál's fleet goes down and I *really* don't want to stick around for the fallout. There will be no planet, no system where I will find peace. Rezál and the rest of the Rule will torch anything and everything in their way to get to me. And when they do—well, it's safer to die.

The easiest way to assure that my kill switch will work is to insert it right into my own brainstem. When my brain dies so will every single fighter under Rezál's command. It might not end the war, but it will turn the tables in favour of the breakaways. It's the best I can do with what I have.

This is a good plan, a *great* plan, a plan I've been mulling over for nearly a decade. Yet, in all my time fantasising about leading the Third Daughter to the slaughter, I never anticipated just how much I would enjoy her company. A pity, really.

The decoding takes all of three seconds. Rezál would have been able to do it herself if she was had been paranoid enough do a full body scan on me. If she did, she couldn't have missed the keys I implanted into my left forearm.

By the time I am once again seated in the Third Daughter's dining room, she's had the decoded schematics for nearly an hour. Given her technical know-how and current overall condition, I'd say she's made absolutely nothing of the blueprints I've given her.

When the Third Daughter collapses on the chair adjacent to mine, I shove my hands below the runner. The bandages around my wrists will most definitely start a conversation I'm not interested in having, and there's also a surprise I'm currently clenching in my right fist. But I must be patient. "Long day?" I ask.

Rezál doesn't bother looking at me. With her habitual detached expression she reaches for a salad fork and twirls it in her fingers. She stabs the greens three times.

The food before us is fresh, succulent. The unexpected benefit of being Rezál's captive is eating *real* food. I haven't had an actual vegetable in years before I landed myself on the mothership. Now it's nearly all I eat. But where has it come from? The ship's own hydroponics or a tropically-inclined planet two gates away? I wouldn't be surprised if this particular green was shipped here because it was Rezál's favourite.

"Not hungry, ma'am?" My own appetite is waning.

Rezál releases her fork and gifts me a long, languished look. "About today," she says, wearily.

Oh, is the Third Daughter suffering from a guilty conscience? "No harm done, ma'am. I should know better than to keep things from you."

She sets her jaw. "It's this damn war. It's pushing me too far."

"It could end today, if you wished it, ma'am." I'm feeling daring as I clench the surprise in my palm.

Rezál, the brilliant Third Daughter, immediately hears me. Her whole demeanor changes and at once she is collected and glacial. "And what good would that bring to the outer systems, Ms. Kato? Before the Rule came upon them, they were nothing more than isolated industrial outposts." She lets out a small, satisfied grin. "They were burning their natural resources for energy. They *grew* their food. *Outside.*"

"And that is—?"

Rezál sneers. "Deplorable. Disgusting. *Uncivilized.*"

"And did they know it was *uncivilized* before the Rule came upon them?"

Rezál opens her mouth to respond, but nothing comes out. She looks down at her salad, most assuredly not grown aboard this ship. Neither is the wine made aboard. Neither is the tablecloth. Everything along this table is borrowed if not stolen. She stabs a small red vegetable with her fork, pouts. "The Rule stabilized the outer systems." She never says *I,* she never says *we.* "It brought them into the network."

Maybe Rezál is right, and the Rule has done more good than harm. Who am I to say? All I know is that my great-grandmother grew her food outside and that we had animals, and festivals, and forests that spanned half the continent. And no one dictated how much of what crop was grown, nor where it was to be transferred. No one told us what to sing or how to sing it. If we were uncivilized, we were also happy in our ignorance.

I also know that when the time came, the system assimilated willingly and without bloodshed. In the end, it didn't matter. The Rezáls made their call, and my home became nothing but a molten sphere, now orbiting another, larger molten sphere. Thanks, Second Daughter and your underdeveloped prefrontal cortex.

"And surely there will be unrest if the Rule falls, and there will be bloodshed." I think about Kaya, about the home our ancestors shared. I think about Shay, from the same system. We gravitated towards one another because each of us carried pieces of cultures and languages, and customs, that were mostly extinct, eradicated. We held on to them as long as we could, before we, too, forgot.

How is it that Kaya can kill so easily when it could be one of ours on the other side? Certainly, Shay has interrogated many from our home system.

"The Rule will not fall," Rezál says, like a doctrine, eyes poised on an orange leaf in the middle of her plate.

"Of course." It's as good time as any to steer the conversation. "Did you have a chance to look at the schematics, ma'am?" I push my chair out. Rezál is still picking away at her salad. She hums affirmative and stabs at the leaf, never once lifting the fork to place anything into her mouth.

"Did it remind you of anything?" I tread softly. She must hear my steps against the carpet, but she doesn't seem to care. I clench the surprise in my hand as tightly as my sluggish fingers will allow it. Just a few more seconds. *Patience. Patience.* "Did it remind you of your implants, Ennis?" I unfurl my fingers and press the magnet in my palm against Rezál's neck. Immediately, her posture seizes up, her hands freeze. Like an appliance disconnected from its power source she nearly folds atop the table. The salad fork drops against her plate with a clank. As my fingers float along her skin, she trembles against them. Rezál doesn't say anything, but her breath hitches. I lower my lips to her ear. I've been waiting for this moment for nearly ten years and it's just as delicious as I anticipated. "What was it, C4, C5?" Rezál says nothing. I hope it's not a higher-level injury, as it would severely impair her breathing, and I don't want her dead—not yet.

"I don't fucking know," the Third Daughter hisses. Even beneath the thick fabric of her blues, I can see her bicep flex as she strains to move her arm. Her index finger twitches.

"I would say C6."

"*Fuck you.*"

I press my forehead against Rezál's temple. Her skin is burning against mine and she's beginning to sweat from both fear and the exertion of staying upright. "Oh, you and your sweet nothings." I have to be careful. Even if she's breathing on her own, she'll grow tired quickly. I may have to cut this conversation short.

"If you're going to kill me, kill me now, save the gloating." Rezál is taking ragged breaths between every word, but she's still conscious.

I suspect she can breathe independently, it's a good sign, but I can't risk it. "Can you breathe without the implants?"

She nods slightly.

"What else can you do?"

A sharp exhale. I think that's her way of laughing now that the implants can't help her. I watch Rezál's index finger jump once. "That's it," she wheezes.

"Why didn't you have it regrown?"

Another pathetic laugh from Rezál. "*Time.*" She swallows and it's obvious that the motion comes with great struggle. "Aera killed herself. No thanks to you. I needed to step up. Then it was too late. No time to float around in a med-tank waiting for my spine to grow itself back together."

My hand rests along the curve of Rezál's neck. She probably can't feel it, but I run my thumb along a small scar where the receiver for her implants was inserted. I want to press my lips against it. "Now the implants are seeping poison into your bones."

"They were supposed to be temporary."

"How unfortunate."

Rezál tries to nod again but can't. Her neck muscles strain forward and remain perfectly still. I nuzzle into her hair, and it smells of honey and fresh sweat. The Third Daughter stops breathing for a moment, tries to recoil, and fails. "I understand it now, I see it," I whisper. "You get off on this, you get off on pinning someone to cardboard, like they're a butterfly, trapping them, studying them up close. You watch them squirm. It turns you on."

"Shut up."

"Make me." That's enough for now. The moment the magnet breaks contact with Rezál's skin she gasps for air as the implants restart. She spins around, all rage and fear. There are two wet trails running down her ashen face.

"Unfortunately, you have something I want," I lie. "You can get me flying again, just once, is all I need, and I will end this war for you." I toss the magnet on the floor. "I get no pleasure from seeing you suffer, ma'am. I'm not like you."

But that's another lie. We're all a little like Rezál. Whoever insists that they would wield power fairly and never abuse it, has never had real power bestowed upon them. Power cuts your teeth until they're predator sharp, and then you go hunting. At least Rezál and I are honest in our violence.

Her paralysis gone, the Third Daughter is on her feet, towering over me. She grabs the front of my coveralls with a steely grip and, in spite of what just happened, gives me a rough shake. "You think your little stunt will go unpunished?" Rezál wants to demonstrate power because she's scared. She wants to burn. I will show her that there's nothing left to burn.

"I understand, ma'am," I tell her, holding her fury effortlessly. "What will you do, Third Daughter, Eternal Rightful? Will you break my limbs or fry my brain? Will you take the thing I cherish most away from me? Will you take my loved ones? Will you burn my home to the ground?" Rezál's grip loosens. "Will you scar my face and send me back to my shithole apartment to rot until my dying days?"

She will see her own despair mirrored in me, her own loss. She will mistakenly believe that we are the same, that we feel the same, suffer the same. She will imprint on me like a baby animal, motherless and helpless. She'll lean on me, and she'll trust me, and that's exactly what I want.

Rezál's hand falls from my coveralls. She kneels and picks up the magnet from the floor. Holding it between her index finger and her thumb, she twirls it in the light. Tenderly, she takes my hand, fingers gentle around the fresh bandages. She lingers, just for a second, and drops the magnet into my palm.

Without a single word she walks past me and out the dining room. The board all set, the opening complete, we move into the middlegame.

THE MIDDLEGAME

NINE

PILOTS ARE A loud lot. They always sit together and brag about a mission they flew and their kill stats.

Someone else will undoubtedly mock the speaker and their kill stats, and propose their own, more impressive ones. The whole thing is bothersome and juvenile. But sometimes things go wrong, and pilots lose their edge and get into all sorts of moods.

That's why today Kaya is eating alone beside *Iron Fox*. She sits cross-legged on the floor, her helmet an arm's reach away. A long tangle of wires reaches from the cockpit to the plug in the back. With a scrunched nose, Kaya digs through what looks like a standard ration of protein and fibre. She doesn't hear me over the general hum of the hangar and her own moping.

"Tough day?" I ask and Kaya recoils hard enough for her back to slam against her fighter. She doesn't answer and only scowls at me with protein in her teeth. "How's Shay?"

"Fuck you, Nez." Kaya scrambles to her feet. "Everything was fine before you got here."

"You mean fucking the Third Daughter behind Shay's back? That was going fine?" I'm in the sort of mood where I want to start a fight, but I also don't want to be blamed for starting said fight. I'm just going to poke Kaya a little, for old times' sake.

Nearly half a head taller than me, she can be quite intimidating, especially this up close. It takes Kaya a single step to invade my space. She grabs the front of my coveralls.

"You sure that's a good idea?" I ask her.

"You caught me off guard earlier. It didn't count."

I toy with the idea of kicking Kaya again, but I'm far more curious about why she's eating all alone apart from her fans. "Why so glum?"

She gives me a good shake. "None of your business."

"Did the Third Daughter spank you harder than usual?"

That does it. Kaya spins us around and slams me against the fighter. My head bounces off the hull with a low thud.

"Or not hard enough?"

"*Shut up,*" Kaya hisses and tightens the grip on my coveralls. Our eyes meet and hers are ablaze with rage. I raise my eyebrows and wait. It takes all of ten seconds for Kaya's features to soften. "She hasn't spoken to me in days. Hasn't called on me, hasn't flown with me. Not since you've come around."

I leave one eyebrow up. "You mean not since you fired on her during a *game*?"

The last of the anger is gone and Kaya effortlessly slips back into self-pity. "I lost it, okay? I was tired and she wanted to play, and I couldn't say no. I just *lost* it."

"She got hurt, you know."

Kaya lets go of my coveralls. She takes one step back. "She doesn't tell me shit, Nez. Not when it matters."

So, the stellar ace of the Rule lost it during a game and fired on her superior (and lover). She then, not a day later, had to face the fact that she wasn't as good as she thought she was. Now, Kaya is left with a shaken confidence and an absent superior (and lover). I almost feel sorry for her.

"Like I said, everything was fine before you got here."

That doesn't feel nice. I should leave it alone. I should leave Kaya alone, but the history is there, the nostalgia is there. It all simmers together in a mixture of jealousy and familiarity, and I dislike it greatly. It feels like not too long ago it was Kaya and I who were lovers, who were having fights. It seems so close. I can't help but go and pick at that scab. It's only natural, isn't it? To want to know about your replacement?

"How did it—how did it happen?"

Kaya doesn't answer right away. She leans against the fighter's hull beside me and walks her feet far enough ahead that our eye levels match. "I wasn't brown nosing, if that's what you're implying."

I shrug. I wouldn't put it past her. Being on every propaganda poster helps a soldier, builds up their name. When the war is inevitably over (or Kaya can no longer fly like yours truly) she'll have something to fall on. Kaya is gorgeous, sure, but her proximity to Rezál helps tremendously with her post-fleet opportunities. She can pretend she wasn't brown nosing, but we both know it wasn't all innocent.

"It was a sort of natural thing. We started flying together. I wasn't right in the head when I got here. Not after what happened with you. I was jumpy, I didn't really trust myself in a fighter. And Rezál, well, she can make you feel like—"

"—like you're the center of the universe?"

"Yeah." Kaya throws me a quick side-glance. "We didn't do anything for two, maybe three years, but you know how it is. You get so comfortable with someone, you trust them, then something shitty happens, something only they will understand. You find yourself at their door and it's the most natural thing ever. It just works. It makes you feel seen."

"She does make you feel seen." I try not to sound sarcastic.

"Yeah." Kaya picks at her nails, roughly. "I owe her my sanity. She's solid. Rezál."

I should leave it there, but that wouldn't be me. After a long enough pause, I gather up enough courage. "Why didn't you ever visit, Kaya?"

She pulls on a hangnail and hisses, puts the finger in her mouth. I can't help but follow it to Kaya's full lips. It takes most of my self-control not to kiss her. Nostalgia is a bitch and I never got closure. "I did, once. Shay and I did. You were in therapy. It must have been early. You couldn't even walk on your own. We didn't think you'd get like—" she motions to all of me. "—like this. *Better.* I couldn't bear seeing you so helpless."

That must have been excrutiating for you, asshole. I spent too many nights believing she'd come, believing that she'd get me out of that hospital and take me home. I spent too much time praying for it to every single deity I could remember and none that I actually believed in. The urge to kiss Kaya seeps away. It trickles down the back of my throat, through my chest, and settles in a cool puddle in the pit of my stomach. The cold echoes through my bones.

I push off the fighter hull. "Don't worry, Rezál will call for you."

"Nez?"

I don't bother turning around. I give Kaya a wave. "We're good. No harm done."

She doesn't come after me as I leave the hangar.

When I return to my workspace, there's a standard ration box waiting for me on the floor. The unappetizing non-perishables have been replaced with whatever Rezál and I were going to have for dinner if I didn't decide to prove a point. I take a still warm dinner roll and bite into it viciously.

A crisp, white paper peers out from the box:

It may appear that at the center of our galaxy there is a blinding star, a single source of all light, when in reality, it is millions of stars. And when you look past those, you will see that it is a gargantuan black hole that keeps everything revolving in its rightful place.

Do not confuse me for the black hole, Ms. Kato, when I am but a mere pulsar, subject to gravitational pull, as all things are.

-Ennis

Rezál's impeccable handwriting stretches the ink evenly across the ivory stationary, signature as short as the leash she claims to be on. I read the note again, bring the paper up to smell it. It still carries the honeyed notes that surround the Third Daughter. Then, I tear it to shreds and throw it into the trash. I drown it in not a small amount of stale coffee for good measure.

I hope you're watching.

I pick an apple from the ration box and eat that too. By the time I eat my way through the dinner contents, my eyes are stinging with fresh tears. I want nothing more than the coffee-stained note in my hand. I want Rezál's glacial eyes on mine. I want her fingers tracing along every wound she leaves on me. At least she has the decency to be honest in her violence, to show her intent when she dispenses hurt. To hell with *Do not attribute to malice what can be explained by ignorance.* To hell with passive slights. The Third Daughter speaks my name like it is danger, a compliment of the highest order. Yes, we will be each other's ends, but we'll look one another in the eye when the final blow comes down. Rezál may be cruel, but she is not indifferent.

To hell with gentle ways.

I WAKE UP to a song I haven't heard in ten years. When we were still together, Kaya used to sing it to me when I was struck with frequent bouts of insomnia. A weepy little tune. It didn't help me sleep, but it was a nice way to pass the time.

For too long, I lie in my cot and listen to her sing. The hollow space carries her voice effortlessly, note after note, through the walls. *And the winter rains shall carry you home.* With a groan, I rock upright and slip my coveralls on. *And the fire will burn bright. And you'll see it from the hills.* I slide the door open as quietly as possible.

"And the door will always be open," Kaya's voice dies to a whisper. She sits in the middle of the empty room, a glowing hologram of the Dragonfly implant swirling above her. Her silhouette dwarfs in comparison to the projections. She pulls her knees to her chest and hugs them. "I just finished a dry run," she says softly, like she's speaking to the room and not me at all. "Thought you'd still be awake."

That explains the flight suit.

"It's very late."

Kaya keeps looking up at the hologram, the faint glow flickers in her irises. "I'd say it's early."

We watch the hologram spin for a few minutes, in complete silence. If memory serves me right, we used to spend hours in each other's space, without saying a single word, enjoying the proximity. Those days were simple: make the bed, get food, train for hours in sim. When sim was down for maintenance or another pilot beat us to the best training times, we'd just lie in my single cot, only mentioning the strange figures we could make out in the peeling barrack ceiling.

"Is this supposed to help us with our hit ratios?" Kaya asks. She was always the first to break any silence.

"It is." I shouldn't tell her anything more, but if she guesses it, Rezál can't blame me. The cameras above us watch the interaction with their glowing red eyes. Nothing goes unnoticed. Nothing will ever be a secret again.

"And this—this thing. It goes where?"

"Your brain."

Kaya recoils from the projection and stares at me in shock. She's doe-eyed and looking for reassurance, not something I can give her. "You can't be serious," she says. "Ennis wouldn't put this—this thing in my head."

"So, you do call her Ennis." I give one of the cameras a *look*. "And she would." She *will*. How I want to tell Kaya everything, every excruciating detail. I want to take her somewhere, where we can be truly alone, free from the Third Daughter's gaze. I want to tell her *everything*. I want to tell her just how much I missed her, and I hated her, and everything in between.

Kaya scrambles to her feet. "I won't have this thing shoved into me."

"You will." I approach her slowly, mimicking Rezál's predatory gate. "You'll do as she says because you're a good soldier and because you're devoted to her. You'll do anything she asks of you. You'll fly headfirst into battle, into certain death, if she tells you to."

"I trust her." Kaya squares her jaw, her voice pitching into a warning.

Oh really? I've struck a nerve. "Suppose you love her more than you've ever loved me." It would be effortless to surrender Rezál's secrets right this instant, to sour whatever closeness they've cultivated. It's tempting to sow despair everywhere I go. So *very* tempting.

"I do."

And just like that, there's closure. Instantaneous, like severing a gangrenous limb in a single slice. Like firing a torpedo on an unarmed vessel. In one swift motion, Kaya's words hit their mark. I expect hurt, but all there's left is hollowness. A small ache spreads from the base of my skull down my neck and through my left arm, familiar, oddly comforting. "Figured."

This will be the last time I speak with Kaya, but I don't

know that. I don't say goodbye. I miss that opportunity. "It's still a ways from being ready, the implant, I wouldn't worry just yet."

But she does worry. I see the fear spread across her perfect features. "And this is supposed to make us *better*? Better pilots?"

It doesn't matter if it does. What matters is that Rezál thinks it does. In the end, the Dragonfly implant is just the same as Rezál's spinal implants. It's a device aimed at fulfilling duty, a crutch, a last attempt. It's the age-old dedication to making people better, forcing them to accomplish more than they are capable of. Even if Rezál sees the parallels, I doubt she'll let it get in the way of her quest for victory. "It'll make piloting easier for you," I tell Kaya.

"You'll make sure it's safe." More of a statement than a question. Kaya is relieved I've let the interpersonal stuff go, deciding not to press. To press, past the reasonable, that would be so me, so *Nez*. Kaya wants specifics, she wants concrete guarantees. I understand that now. She needs someone to tell her the play, the steps, to promise an outcome. A nearly dead (but not quite) pilot in a field hospital is short on guarantees. I understand that now.

I give her a reassuring nod, she matches it. Before she leaves, already standing in the doorways, she calls to me, "I'm still glad you got—" she gestures to all of me, "—that you got better."

And at last, I have nothing left to say to her. "I'm glad too."

TEN

WHEN A DOCTOR tells you that something will only hurt a little— a little pinch, a little jab— it usually means it's going to hurt a whole lot. When a fleet medic tells you that something will only hurt a little, it usually means you will most assuredly black out from the pain. When a fleet medic tells you that something is a bad idea, it means suicide.

Captain Varda looks from me to the three-dimensional hologram of the piloting implant. "I'm not doing this," she says, frigid. "I'm not voluntarily leaving your brain damaged."

"You had no problem shoving that little shocker into my brain."

Varda loses composure for a moment but collects herself with military precision. "And what makes you think that was me?"

"Going to take a gander that you're the only surgeon on deck."

She doesn't deny it. "Best surgeon this side of the gates though."

Oh, I sure hope so.

Varda's not wrong about my piloting implant though. The chances of me walking away from this *at all* are slim, let alone functional. Unfortunately, there's no other way. I know, I checked. My outcome doesn't look good, but I need that implant in my brain sooner than later. "What can we do to increase the odds of survival?"

Varda moans and spins the hologram with her index finger. "This is too clunky. I can't shove this inside your skull and expect it to work. Can you make internal sensors wirelessly connect to the receiver? Saves us space."

"Increases the lag."

"Being brain-dead increases the lag."

She makes a good point. Maybe I shouldn't have been avoiding doctors for the past decade under the impression that their advice is generally useless.

"What is this for, anyway?" Varda asks as she sips coffee from a standard field thermos.

"Military secrets."

She snorts and offers up her thermos, I politely decline.

"Love military secrets," she says and gulps down a mouthful. She switches between spinning the hologram and casting long glances my way.

When this goes on for a solid three minutes, I snap. "*What?*"

"People are talking. Rumours, you know."

People always talk, that's why I try to tune them out most of the time. But given my current position, I'll take gossip. "What kind of rumours?"

"That you're the one who leaked the schematics to the breakaways."

"You really think if I was the one who leaked the schematics, I'd be alive right now? Think the Third Daughter would have that?" I motion for Varda to hand me the thermos. To my pleasant surprise, it's straight bourbon. Above us are at least three cameras. I give one a playful wink. I haven't seen Rezál in nearly three days. I hope she's still watching.

"She's done questionable things before," Varda hums. "Look," she says, taking the thermos back, "I don't care who you are. When you're in here, you're safe. I took an oath, but everyone out there didn't. I'd just be careful with this." She motions to the hologram.

Of course, I'll be careful. I give her a small nod. Since I'm here though— "If you're in a charitable mood, doc, would you dispense me something for my pain? The old arm is acting up and messing with my work."

Varda gives me a look over. "What kind of something? I have everything from *don't operate heavy machinery* to *don't remember your own name*."

I like Varda. When the Rule collapses, I hope she gets out in time and makes a new life as a community doctor on a planet far, far away. I hope she gets to have a cozy little house with a warm little kitchen. "Give me something along the lines of *I need to remind myself how to breathe*."

Varda nods thoughtfully. She rattles around the cupboards and sifts through some pouches and soon produces a small vial filled with a cloudy liquid. "Take a drop, sublingually when the pain gets too much. Not sure if you'll be able to stay upright, but you definitely won't feel anything. Probably shouldn't take it on an empty stomach, but I'm not your mom."

"I'll settle for a cool aunt." I give my thanks and fold up the hologram.

A wireless transmitter wouldn't be the worst idea. It would present a minimally invasive surgery and a faster recovery time. It would speed up the uptake process, which means more pilots could be equipped with it in a shorter amount of time. It sounds like a win-win. Except that the only wireless transmitter/receptor pairing I'm currently in possession of is the one in Rezál's spine.

I don't think she'll let me pull it out and play with it, but I've been wrong before.

Walking around in my coveralls is easy. Most officers and pilots think I'm a tech deserving of very little attention, and most techs, in reality, keep to the hangars. Unnoticed, I climb a flight of stairs and turn left through a long corridor towards the living quarters. The coveralls make me invisible, and so, with the wonderfully potent painkiller in my handy little vial, I make it all the way to Rezál's quarters undetected. I find the door slightly ajar, which in itself is alarming enough.

The Third Daughter doesn't bother turning towards the door as I walk through it. She's hunched over at the corner of her bed, her jacket discarded, her dress shirt flung open. Even from the doorway I can see fine beads of sweat scatter across her nearly grey cheeks. She's in agony and she's been vomiting again. Acid radiates from her bathroom.

I clear my throat. She raises a single finger to stop me from speaking. Despite her silent protest, I cross the room and take a seat beside her on the bed. I place the vial in her clammy palm. "From Varda."

Rezál gives a panicked look.

"I told her it was for me." That gets her to relax. Rezál tries to work the cap herself, but her fingers are far too shaky. *Fine.* I take the vial back and unscrew the lid with my teeth. Lodging the vial between my knees, I fill the pipette and hold it out. "Open your mouth."

The ever-petulant Rezál scowls.

"Come on, you can be all fearless and intimidating when it kicks in."

She reluctantly parts her lips. Once the medicine is in her mouth it begins to act almost immediately. Rezál's breathing slows and the tension falls away from her hands and shoulders. As her balance falters, she leans a little too far forward and collapses, headfirst, into me. With her forehead pressed against my shoulder, she says, "Kaya hasn't stopped by at all."

I stow the vial away. I can't sit there forever, but Rezál's weight barely registers. I place my palm against her back. She's gotten so thin in the past few weeks I can count the vertebrae through the dress shirt by touch alone. I run my fingers along the bony protrusions. "You didn't call for her."

"I shouldn't have to."

"And how do you feel about all that, ma'am?"

Rezál makes a small sound, something between a scoff and a sob, and nothing more. I rub circles along the small of her back. She doesn't say or do much after that, but when I think she's gone and fallen asleep, she asks, "Why won't this body die?"

Because all the wonders of modern medicine were deployed to resurrect you, Third Daughter, so you could carry out the word of the Rule. But I can't answer that and keep my head. There's only so much honesty I can dispense.

"I was supposed to die on impact, Ms. Kato. You were correct, C6, complete. Who lives through that? In a field hospital? The surgery for the implants, I was supposed to die. And afterwards? They gave me five years with these damn things. Why can't this body stop? Why won't it give up?"

Folklore has it that the First Daughter gets all the smarts, and the second Daughter gets all the strength, and the Third Daughter gets the luck. Although, I feel that now isn't a good time to bring it up. Rezál is disgustingly pitiful when she's in pain. "Because you're not giving up." It comes out before I can stop the words.

Rezál nuzzles deeper into me. Her lips brush my clavicle. "You say the kindest things, Ms. Kato," she whispers. "It's all such a shame. You could have been my favourite pilot. You could have been so many great things." Her fingers brush my left arm, trail from the shoulder down to the wrist, and stop at the bandages.

"You could have been dead," I say.

The Third Daughter's lips stretch into a smile against my skin. Her teeth graze against an old bruise. "We never get what we want, do we?"

No, *we* don't. Just as Rezál will not receive the victory she craves, just as I will never fly, will never return home, will never hold Kaya again. "We get what we deserve, ma'am."

"And in your eyes, I deserve to suffer, don't I?"

"How very melodramatic of you, ma'am." I rest my head against Rezál's. Even in her deplorable state, she still smells of honeyed sweetness. I can't keep lying, so I don't. I just keep running my hand against her back, hoping it's distracting enough. For a while it suffices and the Third Daughter drifts off into a shallow sleep. Soon after, sleep takes me too. I can't remember the last time that I slept this deeply, without being knocked out by a sedative.

In our slumber, we sink into the bed. When I peel my eyes open, Rezál's forehead presses into my chest as she snores softly. She has wrapped her arms and one of her legs around me. Of all the sensations I've had the pleasure of experiencing in the past weeks, this is not the worst. Watching her sleep peacefully, it's easy to forget that the Third Daughter has personally taken the lives of hundreds if not thousands, and that's by her own hand.

I'm about to do the same. What's the difference, really?

"If only you were anyone else," I whisper, and the words are drowned out by a rising klaxon.

Rezál shoots up in an instant, eyes ablaze. "Call main deck." The ship's operating system responds with a click and the room floods with low chatter and a dozen overlapping voices. "Update." She shoves me aside, reaches for her jacket.

"Ma'am, we are detecting a carrier-size hostile approaching."

"ETA?"

"T-minus twenty, ma'am."

Rezál is already on her feet, jacket done up to the tip of the collar. "Why wasn't it detected earlier?"

"Ma'am, it just exited the gate."

Rezál freezes with one foot in her foot, the other, bootless and in the air. I watch her come to the same horrid realization that I am also coming to. The ship is coming from the gate *behind* us. It means that one of the systems closer to the center has broken off. The fractures in the Rule are spreading, eating their way towards the heart.

"Prepare to launch fighters. I'll be up in three." She turns to me, a small grin stretching along her lips. "Come watch us play. It will be useful for your work."

Play. A chill shakes me. Not two minutes ago, I held Rezál close, deluding myself into thinking that she could be reasoned with, that she could be talked down from this bloodshed. Now, the Third Daughter relishes in war.

"Right behind you, ma'am." Yet, I can never say no to Rezál's invitations. She extends them with the same abandon whether dinner or the slaughter of a whole carrier. I'd follow her bloody invitations to hell.

I expect the main deck to be a cacophony of panic, but when we get there, I am greeted with neat rows of technicians at their consoles. The main deck's curved ceiling sits at least twenty feet up from the floor. A handful of deck engineers are huddled together behind large screens around the edges. At the center, a three-dimensional hologram of the first one-hundred kilometers of flight space hovers right above its table projector.

The moment we step inside, Rezál fires off commands, in a level but demanding voice. "I need updates on the hostiles. Expected number of fighters in flight space. I need updates on our own fighters. Patch *Iron Fox* directly to me, everyone else stays online with dispatch."

A low *yes, ma'am* calls back from the consoles. No one looks up from their workstations to notice me, so I stay by Rezál's side as she spins the hologram around, studies it from every angle. Her eyes race along every outline as she calculates every possible outcome, prepares to jump at any opportunity for victory.

"Everyone is oddly calm, given the situation."

Rezál scoffs, her eyes glued to the projection. "We are the largest carrier the Rule has. Our shields are charged to maximum. We can take hundreds direct hits. This is just—" Rezál presses her finger to the receiver in her ear. "Kaya, be ready to deploy in five. We'll run the Bait and Switch. Hang back until my order. Feel free to pick off any stragglers but don't go in too hot. Understood? No, no sacrifice, not today. Save it for an actual fight."

"What's the Bait and Switch?" *We don't do sacrifices anymore* my ass.

The Third Daughter gives me a chilling Cheshire smirk. "Stick around and find out."

The next ten minutes are a blur. Rezál gives commands without breaking away from the hologram while she rotates the image with her index finger. Every once a while, she speaks directly into her earpiece, a fragile lifeline to *Iron Fox* herself. On the other end of the line, I hear Kaya's faint voice as she leaves the hangar and directs herself and a quarter of the mothership's fighters towards the hostiles. Her fighter and about four dozen others appear on the holographic projection.

"I expect to make a quick exercise of this," Rezál muses, her face a glow with the faint light of the hologram. "I'd like to extend an invitation to dinner, Ms. Kato."

"Is that an order?" There are too many moving parts, too many things to keep track of. I'm losing my bearings, unlike Rezál who seems completely at home.

"An invitation. You may decline if you desire."

She's never worded it like that before, the option to decline. But like I said before, I would follow her invitations to hell.

The hologram flickers. The hostiles have entered the dreaded hundred-kilometer flight space. Rezál mutters into her earpiece and then addresses the deck. "I want everyone awake. Shields up. We're playing the standard

Bait and Switch. I want everyone ready."

A chorus of *yes, ma'am* erupts. No one looks up from their stations. Only the sound of typing hands breaks through the deadly silence on deck.

"Numbers?" Rezál calls out.

"We have fifty out on the field. Sitting at a one-to-one ratio. No attempts at a direct hit—" the tech breaks off mid-sentence as the hull vibrates beneath our feet, "—correction, ma'am. One attempt at direct hit. Shields taking it well."

Rezál nods. "Keep updating me on ratios."

"You're planning to take them out in individual dogfights?" I ask, disturbed by my own curiosity.

Rezál only smiles. "We'll hang to the periphery and pick them off one by one. I'm not in the mood to waste resources."

I watch as the battle unfolds on the hologram. Rezál's fighters are taking losses, but for every one of the Rule's fighters, they take down one of the breakaways. The cruiser itself is only a quarter size that of the mothership, it doesn't have reserves. As the fight continues, one pilot hangs back and takes shots on the breakaways that get a little too far.

"Five is not bad," Rezál mutters into her headset.

Then, one of the techs snaps their head back. "Ma'am," she cries out. "Incoming communication from the cruiser."

Gracefully, Rezál throws me a look over her shoulder. "And now we bait. Patch it through." The Third Daughter pivots towards a new hologram, this one projected at a real-life scale. A man in his fifties appears dressed in a khaki uniform. From his weathered face and the stretched skin along his cheeks, I can tell that he's flown, a lot.

"Greetings, Third Daughter, Eternal Rightful."

To my surprise, Rezál gives him a little bow. "Greetings, Vice-Admiral Yueh. I thought I recognized that cruiser from somewhere. You didn't bother painting over the crest?"

Did the cruiser belong to the Rule? Did Yueh desert?

"It seems only yesterday you were a child, Third Daughter, hiding under the table while we had dinner."

"It seems only yesterday that Mother trusted you with your own armada," Rezál says, steel in her voice. "I see you've bet against her, and you've bet wrong."

It's now Yueh's time to bow. There's history there, kind history, which makes it that more difficult for Rezál. Her own Vices are joining the very rebellion she is tasked to squash.

"You've got us outgunned, Third Daughter. I'd like to extend an offer of surrender before things get unnecessarily bloody."

There's a predatory spark in Rezál's eyes. "I'd like to accept your offer, Yueh." She throws her techs a look. "As a gesture of goodwill, lower your shields, and we will board. Starting with the *Iron Fox*, you remember her."

Yueh nods and throws Rezál a salute. "You are kind Third Daughter, much kinder than your predecessor. We wait to receive the *Iron Fox*."

The entire exchange is too simple, too transparent. It makes no sense even to a military novice like myself. Why exit a gate with guns ablaze when you are clearly no match for the mothership? Why engage in a dogfight you would lose? There is nothing more suspicious than an easy victory. Is Rezál paying attention? *No.* Rezál is still too doped up to think clearly. Her pupils are still dilated. She doesn't see it coming, the trap.

Rezál cuts the transmission. "And receive they shall," she proclaims, voice rising. "Their shields?"

"Lowered, ma'am."

"Ma'am?" I try to get Rezál's attention.

The Third Daughter turns to me, a triumphant smile playing on her lips. "And now, we switch."

She touches her earpiece and speaks to Kaya directly now: "Deliver the payload."

"Ma'am, it's not safe."

Rezál ignores me, far too focused on the floating hologram.

"I think this is a trap," I try again, but Rezál's eyes are poised on the hologram in anticipation. My words fall on deaf ears. "They're not here to win, they're here to take Kaya out."

The next minute blurs into a nauseating panic. Not a second after Rezál gives her order, the fighter that has been hanging back changes course right towards the hostile's cruiser. In the next moment, a projectile is released. The Vice-Admiral's cruiser disappears from the projections.

"And that's Bait and Switch," she proclaims triumphantly as the deck erupts in cheers. I don't hear the acclaim. My ears ring, louder and louder until there's no other sound but it. Before I manage to turn away, I empty the contents of my stomach on the deck floor. *It's a trap, it's a trap, it's a trap.* Lesser things have turned the tides. Lesser things have destroyed morale and ended battles, and Kaya is not some *lesser* thing. Kaya is the face of this fleet. Taking her out would land a devastating blow to the Rule. *Run Kaya, run.*

"Get Kaya out of there," I say, but my words are drowned out by the cheers.

Rezál turns to me. Her face is solemn, cut from weathered stone of a shoreline. "That's war, Ms. Kato. It's not fair, it's only—" she breaks off, spins towards the hologram. "What do you mean?" with a flick of a wrist she magnifies the projections. One of her fighters is pursued by two torpedoes. "When did they have the chance to—? No—no, you're fast." She spins the hologram around. "No. Just breathe. Don't panic. Our shields can take it, you just can't break your speed. Trust me, you got this." Rezál calls out to the techs, "I need support for *Iron Fox*. Two torpedoes on her tail. Needs assist."

I push past the nausea and towards the table projector. The gap between Kaya's fighter and the torpedoes is closing.

"We practiced this, just stay calm and trust in me," Rezál mutters into the earpiece. "Just roll and—"

Without a warning, a third torpedo appears on the projection. For just a moment there are four objects, frozen in the image's center, and then they're all gone, erased from existence. The deck is silent. They were just there. Kaya was just there. Where—where has she gone?

Rezál braces against the table's edge, knuckles white.

Where did the third torpedo—

Rezál takes a deep, shuddering breath.

Where is Kaya? Where is—

"*Iron Fox* has taken a direct hit. Fighter and pilot are destroyed." Rezál's knee buckles and she sags forward against the table. "Tally up our losses. Forward the numbers to my quarters."

Where is—

From here on there's only blood. Blood pounding at my ears. Blood smeared across Rezál's face as I break her nose. I throw her back against the table projector. She doesn't put up a fight. I strike her once, twice. The second blow lands across her cheekbone, but she doesn't even wince. I strike her once more before the techs pull me off. Someone is bending my arm too far back, but I don't care. Break my arms, break every bone in my body. Just return her to me. Just give me back Kaya.

"How could you miss this? How could you think it would be this easy?" I can shout all I want, but it's done. Time is linear, there's no undoing it.

Kaya, Kaya, I taught you how to do your first barrel roll. I taught you to sing all the dirty limericks. Where did you go? Why won't you come back? I held you so close. I held you the best that I could. Why did you leave? Why did you leave for this place and devote your life to the wrong side? Why did you put your trust in *her*?

"Please, take Ms. Kato back to her quarters." Rezál pushes off the table. Her voice reaches me through a fog. The Daughter's face is pale underneath the fresh crimson. More of it runs down her chin, stains her blues. Her bottom lip quivers, but she wills it still. "Make sure she has everything she needs to continue her work."

As the techs push me out the door, Rezál crouches by the table. She loses her balance and tumbles forward, her forehead making rough contact with the floor. Her shoulders shudder through the uniform, just barely.

No one is there to pick her up.

ELEVEN

HALFWAY THROUGH THE sleep cycle, a phantom shadow lurks in my doorway. A tattered ghost of the Third Daughter, far too spent to haunt, pays me an unannounced visit. I watch her from my bed without getting up. No, I haven't slept. I don't think I will sleep ever again. I haven't worked. I don't think I will work ever again. I wait for Rezál to say something, but she just stands in the doorway, silent, hollow. Two strips of medical adhesive align her nose. Her left cheekbone, where my fist collided with it not six hours ago, is burgundy. I also somehow managed to split her top lip.

She takes a step into the room, then another. "I lost her too," she says, weakly. She's come without any officers by her side, no help. This isn't a regular exchange of information, neither is it an interrogation. This is personal, quiet, intimate. She's come to me for comfort.

"She wasn't yours." But I would gladly strike her again if only I had anything at all left in me.

"It wasn't how you think." Rezál walks over to the wall, leans against it and lets gravity take her all the way down to the floor. Her blues are flung open, and the once white dress shirt is brown with curdled blood. In the darkness, her eyes glisten with tears. "I saw that she was flying during the sleep cycles. I didn't have anyone to fly with, so I started going out with her." Rezál takes a breath, squeezes her knee with her right hand hard enough for the tendons on her fingers to bulge. "It took me three months to ask her to dinner."

"Order her."

"No, I *asked*. She said it was a bad decision given the difference in our ranks." Rezál throws her head back against the wall. "I agreed. We kept flying. Then Captain Lindin was transferred here, and they started their thing. It wasn't until two years after that she showed up at my door, unannounced. I couldn't say no. I couldn't—she was the only one to call me out regardless of rank. I didn't have it in me to stay away."

A dangerous rage brews in my stomach. "She wasn't *yours*. *Mine*. She was always *mine*."

"Don't delude yourself. Maybe for a year, she was yours. Maybe once upon a time you two were fucking and having a good time," Rezál hisses. "*Six years* she's been by my side, every night. *Six fucking years*. She left you and you never moved past it. That's on you."

The rage simmers. If I'm going to hurt, then the Third Daughter will hurt right by my side. "You think she would have stayed if she knew you were a cripple?"

Rezál chuckles, unfazed. "You think she would have stayed if you weren't?"

"Yes," I shout. "Yes, she would have stayed. She would have never left and never come here, and never given herself to you. She would have been safe. I would have kept her safe. She would still be alive. She would—" And now it's out in the open and it's too late to reign it back.

Accompanying the answer, a wave of sadness pushes fresh tears to my eyes. There are no more words after that. I rake the fingers of my good hand through my hair and yank on it as hard as I can. I want to bargain anything, *everything*, just to rewind the clock, just to tell Kaya to stay. I would trade anything for that.

Rezál rests a heavy hand on my shoulder and then her forehead presses against mine. Her breaths are coming in short gasps, like she's trying her best to keep composure. "You don't have to keep working." she mutters quickly. "You don't have to make better pilots. It's not worth it."

We're close enough for our noses to brush. She smells of sweat and antiseptic. "No," I lie to her. "They killed her. They have to pay."

"And it still won't bring her back." Rezál traces my cheek with the tip of her nose, her lips brush against my skin. I wrap my good arm around her waist and pull her close. She finds rest in the nook of my neck, and I let her cry against me. All I can do is hold her tightly as her slender frame is rattled with silent sobs. I have nothing to say to her, no words of comfort. I dig my fingers into the fabric of her dress shirt and let her release all the misery into me.

"She was *mine*, Nez. She was *mine*," Rezál whispers, over and over again, and I let her, until she falls asleep in my arms.

WHEN THE SLEEP cycle ends, Rezál is still in my cot. She's wrapped herself around me, and even managed to unzip my coveralls in her sleep. One of her hands now rests flush against my ribs and I'd like for it to stay there forever. Her bare feet dangle off the edge. She's far too tall for the cot. I wonder how she ever made it as a private, sleeping in the barracks.

It's Rezál, she was never a private.

I can pinpoint the exact moment the Third Daughter wakes up, when her whole body instantaneously spasms. Then, deliberately, she relaxes each limb and steadies her breathing, as if the former could go unnoticed. She doesn't say anything, but she doesn't pull away. For a moment, she removes her hand from my side, but decides she likes it better there, and eases it flush against my skin.

"Did you sleep?" I ask as if I had.

She pulls herself closer and tilts her face upwards. "For a second I thought it was just a nightmare."

Eyes still puffy and red, Rezál looks up at me like she's praying for me to fix all of this. I can't fix this. I can't raise the dead. "Varda thinks the implant will need to be separated into two parts. I think she's right." I gently detangle myself from Rezál's limbs and crawl off the cot. The more distance I can keep between us, the safer. As long as I can keep moving, keep working, I can shut out the reality of current events. I know I can't run from Kaya's death forever, but just long enough. "Your implants operate by wirelessly transmitting commands across your spine. I'll need the schematics to those. Can you get those, ma'am?"

Rezál sits on the corner of the cot, head hung forward. Her fingers dig into the thin mattress until her skin pales from the pressure. "I'm pulling the plug on your little dragonfly project."

Not good.

"Ma'am?"

When Rezál rises from the cot she makes no more than a rustling sound, the last leaf blown away by autumn's wind. For a moment, her façade cracks and her eyes widen a smidgen as she studies me. Her lips part but she fails to say anything at all. Her right hand trembles and she presses it against her thigh for control.

I understand grief, I do. I understand the fear of the unknown, but Rezál isn't the type to backpedal this quickly.

She's not the type to back away from a fight. Have I been wrong about her this whole time?

"Ma'am, within your timeframe, this is the most assured way to secure a victory."

She looks at me, her gaze is hollow, lifeless. There is nothing beneath the greys of her eyes, no fire, no vengeance. "I'm aware."

Now, I'm worried, for real. Neither of us knows how to proceed. I think it rude to stare at her, so I move to the sink and pretend to wash my face. Rezál collects her jacket from the floor and slides it over her shoulders. My face is safely submerged under an inch of water when the Third Daughter shuts the door behind her.

I can give her a little time to reconsider, to mourn. When the time comes, I can even nudge. But that time needs to come soon. If my plan is to happen, I need most of the fleet's pilots equipped with my dragonfly implant within the next few months. I can't give the Third Daughter the time she needs. I may have to nudge sooner than she's ready.

With nothing more to do, I brush my teeth and drink my first cup of coffee. I fling the images of the dragonfly implant into a three-dimensional projection above me and begin to untangle the schematic in a way that will allow for wireless communication.

I've done similar work before. Last time, it was for a remote-controlled drone that would penetrate ship shields and place explosives directly on to the hull. Rule ship shields are effective against high velocity projectiles, mostly so that they would protect the hull from torpedoes and could still be operational when fighters got launched at lower speeds. But that was one dumb—

Someone clears their throat behind me and causes me to nearly jump out of my boots. I sniff the air. Cheap liquor. Coffee. And of course— "Shay." I don't turn around. I can't deal with *this* right now. Shay's footsteps stop to the right of me.

"How did it happen?" he slurs.

"Knowing won't help anything." I spin the hologram around, praying it will distract me enough, so I don't cry.

"How did it happen?"

I take a slow sip of my coffee to buy myself a second to collect my thoughts. "She couldn't outrun three torpedoes."

"She didn't have help?"

"It was too sudden."

"*Shit.*"

Another sip of coffee buys me a valuable five seconds. Within those five seconds I come up with a new plan. It's a longshot and it's not nearly as good as my previous plan, but this one can go forth without Rezál's involvement. It's desperate and sloppy, but at this junction, what do I have left to lose? First, I need to get Shay on my side. It's not pretty, and it's not honest, but it's going to do the trick.

"Shay, how much do you know about her involvement with the Third Daughter?" Neither of us will say Kaya's name. When you get involved with pilots, you always anticipate this conversation. The *after* conversation. It's still a rough go. I wonder if they ever had this conversation after my crash.

"Not this again."

"Not like that." I finally gather the courage to look at Shay directly. His uniform is flung open, dress shirt stained with spilled liquor. He has this lost expression about him that makes him look like an overgrown pet. One that I should be comforting. "I think Kaya was privy to information that we weren't."

The self-pity dissipates and Shay sobers up instantly. "You already have something in mind." *Oh, do I ever.* But first, we need to find a safe place to speak without Rezál's eyes and ears on us. I grab a stack of note paper from my desk and drag Shay to the hangar.

The noise today is low, energy is equally low. The news of Kaya's passing can't be contained and already they're drawing mourning sigils on the posters. The techs are wearing black armbands. I want them all to stop pretending like they really cared for Kaya, like they knew her, like her posters won't be replaced in three days' time with someone younger, prettier, *new*. I want them all to disappear so that I can set each and every single poster on fire, one by one.

I pull Shay into the shadow of the closest fighter and motion with my chin upwards *climb*. Still a little drunk he starts making his way to the cockpit, wobbling along the rungs. Fighters have streaming cameras inside them, but they're usually turned off, especially during charging. It's a waste of energy to keep them running. This is the only remotely safe place in all of the mothership.

Once inside, I point to the pilot's seat. Very softly, I say, "No talking. I'm going to write things and pass them to you. You write back."

Shay nods.

What does Intelligence and Investigations know about Rezál's health? I scribble and pass it to Shay.

He shrugs and gives me a thumbs up *all good*. I shake my head with a small smile. I have to deliver this just right or Shay will take it straight to the Third Daughter.

She's got six months to live. Less now.

Shay reads the note. Then motions for the pen. In his level handwriting: *proof?*

Kaya had proof.

Shay rubs his face with both hands, willing the last of the alcohol induced fog to lift. Then he starts writing. *Rezál killed—*

He doesn't get to finish. I pull the paper over. *Nothing unusual about a pilot going out in a fight.*

I should take this straight to the Third Daughter and have you executed for treason, Shay writes. He's right, of course, and I am incredibly stupid to come to him with this at all. But stupid is the only option I have left right now. People can be logical, yes, but inherently we're emotional beings.

I'm both emotional and desperate right now, and very much past caring.

I can argue how this all makes sense, but if Shay isn't emotionally invested, it's all moot. I have to make it personal. *The Rule is fracturing. The ship we engaged with was a Rule cruiser, defecting. The Third Daughter is dying, this is a fact, she's desperate for a victory. All of these things are facts! Now that you know the truth, even if you go to Rezál, she will remove you.*

Shay scoffs, but there's fear in his eyes. He knows I'm not fucking around.

You have a choice. Go to Rezál and tell her what you know or start thinking about your after. I know they don't train all your critical thinking out. You're not a regular soldier. You can think for yourself. Think of what you can do with this intel. Think about the damage. Think about how quickly it can end the war, end Rezál.

Proof? Shay scribbles.

I want to stab Stay with the pencil. *I have a contact. Outside. He'll have everything you need.* Even if Shay never meets my contact, never gathers the proof, never broadcasts it to the galaxy, he'll still be out, he'll still be outside Rezál's immediate grasp. That's all I can hope for.

But Shay's not convinced. In the dim fighter cockpit, deep worry lines fold along his forehead. *Why? Why get involved at all?*

Well, you see, you were the one who dragged me out here after disappearing for ten years. I can't tell him that. What good does blame do anyway? Would good would it do to remind Shay that it was him that left the scars along my wrists, when he already has trouble looking me in the eye? What good would it do to ask why he never came around after the accident? He could never fix these things, undo the damage. No one is blameless here. *Because believe it or not I gave two shits about you and Kaya. Even after—* I scribble instead.

"I think I need another drink," Shay says out loud, his voice hoarse and stained.

"Have ten. Hell, drown yourself. Make it look like you're not coping. When your bosses send you on leave, go here." I quickly jot down a name and address and hand it to Shay. I tear out the previous pages and crumple them. Shay instinctively pats the front pocket of his jacket and pulls out a small lighter.

There's nothing flammable in the cabin, so we watch the paper and our communication burn to ash against the floor. When we part ways, neither of us say anything. This is the third-last time I will see Shay, but I don't know it yet.

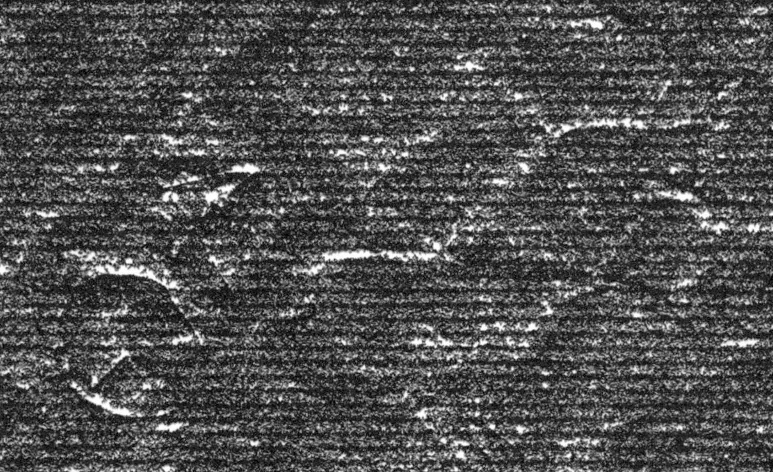

TWELVE

OVER THE COURSE of the next week, I see Shay exactly once. He's drunk and alone at a far table in the officers' mess hall. He's crying and I really don't know, nor do I care, if they're honest tears or not. Intelligence and Investigations, who knows what kind of stuff they do? By the time end-of-day meals finish, Varda comes around and gently leads him away.

In the same week, I see the Third Daughter exactly zero times. When the last hour of the last day draws to a close, I make my way to her quarters. Still in my coveralls, I am invisible to any officer in my way. There are glances, sure, but no one asks anything of me.

The dining room sits empty. Without Rezál present, it's just hollow and dark, just a little unimposing without its main attraction. The Daughters follow me with their painted eyes. Ira Rezál, her long bleached hair braided tight. Her icy glare alone enough to lower the temperature in the room by several degrees. Aera Rezál, her madness palpable even on canvas. And Ennis, young Ennis, already different from her predecessors even in her youth.

She is the only sister to be painted in her dress uniform, rich cream against the dark background. The only sister to be painted with a small smirk on her lips. The potential for something remarkable was there all along, the potential to change the course of Rule history. And yet—

I shut the doors to the dining room and leave the family alone.

No one answers my knocks on the bedroom door. I press my ear to the wood and hear nothing. With only one place left to check I mosey over to the deck.

Half-perched on the projector table, the Third Daughter lazily spins the hologram of some system with her index finger. I spend a few glorious seconds just watching her precise movements, watching *her*. The faint blue of the image dances around in her grey eyes as she leans in closer to study a nameless distant planet. I follow the angle of her jaw as it runs towards her neck, drawing a line all the way to the crisp collar of her blues, where it disappears beneath the heavy fabric.

Rezál catches me staring. The left corner of her lips tugs upwards.

"Axal," she calls out, "take the bridge."

A uniformed officer stirs from the controls at the front. With the same rigid precision, Rezál motions for me to follow her as she moves past me and into the corridor. "It's been a busy stretch," she says when we're out of earshot of the crew. "Systems are breaking off everywhere. I need to decide which way to go, who to chase. Traitors, the lot of them."

We're following the corridor in a direction I've yet to explore. Rezál walks a full length ahead of me, her steps as exact as a metronome.

"And what have you decided, ma'am?"

"Screw it all."

What? "Ma'am?"

Rezál throws me a wistful smile over her shoulder.

"Screw the war. Screw everything." With a wave of her hand, she parts a doorway and steps inside. "I'm tired of this nonsense."

The insides are nearly pitch black, but there's something reflective in here. Light creeps in, enough to play along what seems like a mirror at the far end of the room. Only the sound of Rezál's faint breathing reaches me now, coming from a distance. She's disappearing into the abyss without a word.

That's when the mirror in front of me splits into two halves. It's not a mirror at all, but a window. My breath hitches. I've seen space before. *Real* space. But seeing it like this, while in the middle of it, has a chilling exposure to it. Light from distant stars illuminates the room just enough for me to make out a silhouette by the window.

Rezál rests her forehead along the glass, her fingers trail downwards, tracing the outlines of galaxies and nebulous clusters dozens of lightyears away. "I thought I could end it quickly. I thought Kaya and I could go somewhere and just *be* until it was my time. It got out of hand so fast." Her voice is small, like she is drowning in the cosmos. She lets the silence hang for a few minutes before continuing. "After my crash, Mother visited me, you know. She came all the way from the Center to some field hospital, all to see me. Can you guess what she said?"

"No, ma'am." She's disgustingly pathetic and self-pitying, and I want nothing more than to comfort her.

"She said to get it together."

"And did you?"

Rezál gives a breathy laugh. "What do you think, Ms. Kato?"

I think if what she meant by *getting it together* was murdering thousands of people who stand up against you, then yes, absolutely. Rezál leans against the glass, her whole weight resting through her shoulder. Fine beads of sweat scatter along her forehead.

"I think you're in pain," I say. "I think you're tired."

Rezál winks at me. "Correct," she whispers and rests a heavy hand on my shoulder. "I come here to think sometimes. Kaya really liked it here. It's quiet, it's like a direct line to the universe, she used to say. This used to be a happy place." She takes a ragged breath, and a crack appears in her carefully crafted facade. "I brought you here to say, I don't want to do this anymore."

"The war?"

"The war. The living." Rezál squeezes my shoulder. "I knew it was always a possibility, getting involved with a pilot like that, it's always a possibility, but I never imagined Kaya would meet that fate."

"You thought she was too good."

"I thought I'd take better care of her."

What does she want me to say? "You did the best you could."

But she didn't. She got sloppy, she got careless, and she paid the price. *No.* Kaya paid the price. I brace against the deep gnawing in my chest. There's nothing to be done now, blame won't revive Kaya.

Rezál's eyes meet mine. The faint light from the stars washes her face of any colour. Her blues appear nearly black. Yet, she is far from done. There is still strength in her fingers as she squeezes my shoulder. There is still an edge to her jaw. In these moments, it's easy to forget that she is the Third Daughter. In the moments when she shows weakness, it's easy to fall prey to her vulnerable charm.

"I failed her," Rezál whispers. "I failed everyone." Her hand slides from my shoulder to my neck. Her touch is like the electricity piercing my brainstem again. She leans in and presses her lips against mine, decisively. Rezál pulls the pen at the base of my neck and sends my hair spilling past my shoulders. She smiles against my lips.

Not a month ago I would have—well, according to

many highly inappropriate dreams I've been having about the Third Daughter, I would have had her right there, but the echo of our first encounter, still fresh enough to sting, stops me. No matter how counterintuitive, I gently push Rezál away. Not too far. I want to feel her warmth around me for another second. "Ma'am. You can have any officer, any pilot, with the snap of your fingers. Anyone at all—you can have someone you find beautiful."

"It's not about beauty." She draws back, far enough that I can watch genuine fear spill across her perfect features. Rezál lets her hand fall from my hair and retreats. In moments like these, it's *so easy* to forget. It's so easy to see her pain and want to end it. "You're the only one who knows where I hurt." She's not talking about a failing body. "You're the only one I trust not to take advantage of it."

"Why?"

"Because you hurt just the same."

Well, that does it. We're going to fuck.

I wrap my arm around Rezál's waist and spin her around to press her back against the glass. She's taller, so I raise on my tippy toes to kiss her properly. I'm in awe of how perfectly her narrow frame fits against my broader one, how she arches herself into me as I deepen the kiss. I remove my hand from her waist only to pull away the edge of Rezál's jacket and the dress shirt underneath. I run my fingers along the edge of her trousers, and she moans sweetly into my mouth.

You know when I said that power is a turn-on? Yeah, *that*.

"Not here," she says.

"No," I press her harder against the glass, my pelvis grinds against hers. "Right here. Your help can sew buttons back on, overnight right?"

She nods. *Good*. Despite the thickness of the synthetic wool, I make easy work of every single gold button along the front and send them scattering along the floor. Rezál's dress shirt meets the same fate.

Her hands fumble around with my coveralls. She manages to get the zipper down and then just freezes, not knowing how to slip it past my shoulders. "It's not so difficult," I tell her. The Third Daughter pouts as I slowly slide the material over one shoulder at a time, frustrated by the interlude. "Too quick and my shoulder will pop right out."

"I'll just pop it right back in." She runs her gaze over my body, pausing at times, studying every imperfection. She doesn't say anything, but she doesn't try to make it easy on me. An uncomfortable and unfamiliar feeling stirs in my stomach.

Shame.

Ten years and I've been lucky to avoid it and yet here, with Rezál's complete attention on me, on every last bit of me, it's effortless to fall prey to it. I've never wanted to slink into a dark corner, to cover every inch of skin and hide it from the world, until now. But instead of words, she pulls herself flush against me. "Nez," she whispers, and kisses down my neck and along my bad shoulder. There's a sliver of flesh there, more sensitive than everything else (it's the way the peripheral nerves healed, go figure). When she runs her tongue along it, I nearly lose all sense of composure.

And I want her then in the way a fire wants to burn everything in sight. I want her the way we all want to destroy beautiful things. To be her executioner, to be her salvation, I want it all. I want to taste and hear nothing but Rezál. I want to sink my teeth into her core and tear the livelihood from her.

I guide her down to the floor with me as I fight her trousers off with one hand. I kiss between her breasts and down the flat stomach, along the jagged scar where her shattered instruments perforated a fragile, human body, where steel met flesh after a deadly crash, and I can feel her relax for what seems like the first time in her life. When I graze my teeth across Rezál's hip bone, she gasps and grabs a handful of my hair.

is barely big enough for the five of us to stand inside. It's dark. A two-way mirror separates us from a second space.

My stomach seizes up as I recognize the space.

"I thought you'd recognize it earlier," Rezál muses. "But I suppose you were sedated."

Her words barely register as I stare at the same aluminum table and chair, only this time it's Shay who is tied down. He doesn't appear to be too hurt. Only his eyes, and overall blank expression suggest that he is under the influence of a sedative. They questioned him, that much is certain. I jerk towards the glass but manage to stop myself in time. "You know physical torture won't work, especially on Intelligence and Investigations. They train specifically for this."

Rezál nods. "You're right, but there's nothing that Captain Lindin knows that he hasn't already divulged."

My knees buckle. Of course, Shay talked. *Of course.* A part of me knew this would happen, a part I successfully silenced until now.

"He came straight to me after your little chat," she continues. "Captain Lindin is a good soldier, so he told me everything, in excruciating detail. I really appreciated that."

"Then let him go. He's of no use to you."

One of Rezál's officers hands her a worn leather sheath. Slowly, she pulls a long, curved dagger from it, the handle encrusted with splendid jewels. The faint light dances along the blade like the tongues of a dying fire. "Like you said, Nez, he already knows and that alone means he can't leave here."

I tried to keep them out of the crossfire. I tried to keep them both away, to keep them safe.

One officer grabs my arms and handcuffs them behind my back. My left shoulder screams out in protest, but I silence it. "Ma'am, imprison him, throw him in isolation, but he doesn't deserve to die."

"If only you didn't bring him into this, Nez." Rezál walks through the door to the second room and now my screams can't reach her. And scream I do. All of it, useless. Shay can't hear me. Rezál can't hear me, not that it would sway her decision.

When she comes behind his chair and whispers in Shay's ear, he gives her a curt nod. My knees give away completely. The officer lets me crumble to the floor, but doesn't let go of my shoulders. I'm meant to watch this, every second of it. "No, no, *no*," is all I can whisper as Rezál takes the dagger and drags it along Shay's neck. Not an hour prior, Rezál's hands were on me, gentle and kind, and now, both arteries along Shay's neck are severed and he slumps forward, blood gushing from the wound. He'll be dead in seconds.

When it's finished, Rezál looks up. There's no victory in her eyes as she stares through the mirror and into the very core of me. She looks exhausted. A splash back of arterial blood trickles along her chin, but she doesn't seem to notice. The Third Daughter wipes the dagger on the side of her trousers and returns it to its sheath. My ears are ringing and it's the loudest sound in the world.

"Leave us," she says upon her return, and I'm allowed to finally hit the floor. I press my forehead against the cold steel and pray to disappear. When the officers leave, Rezál reaches for my shoulder, but I flinch away. She grabs a handful of my hair and drags me upright. "Look, *look*," she hisses, her lips grazing my ear. She gives my head a shake for good measure. "Look what you've done. You got *sloppy*. You got *desperate*. You're so disappointing, Nez. You've forced my hand. You've forced me to waste an Intelligence Captain. I'm a fool for thinking you capable of proper sabotage."

Shay, slumped across the metal table, blood pooling at his feet. I shut my eyes, but there's only blood. "Look what *you've* done, ma'am. Your own are deserting, your best pilot is dead. You're losing." It would sound much more damning if I wasn't sobbing between the words.

Rezál puts her weight against me, her anger melting away. "Of all the things you could have used to end me, you told him my secret. I thought we had an understanding."

The way her voice shakes is almost genuine. I want to believe that despite everything, the Third Daughter is still capable of hurt. That below the façade there is a person, a woman, who despite her circumstances still *feels*.

"I didn't just come aboard your ship to fuck you, ma'am."

Rezál relaxes her hand of my hair, but rests it on my neck still. "Of course not," she says and gives me a sad smile. "You came to sabotage my pilots."

There it is, the real reason for pulling the plug on the Dragonfly project.

"How long have you known?" It doesn't matter. It's finished. *I'm finished.* What feels like my last breath leaves my body.

"Right after your meeting with Varda, she caught something in the code that I could never. She really is the best."

"*Fuck you.*"

"You did, and it was—" Rezál hums, "—mediocre."

There's nothing left to say after that. Our confessional drawing to a close, Rezál stands up. She loses her balance and leans against the closest wall. Every move is coming to her with great effort. "This has all been very disappointing, Ms. Kato," she says, "but I am a woman of my word, and I will sacrifice you to bless my victory. Until that moment comes, you will be confined to the brig. I'm sorry, but I cannot let you run around messing with my crew any more than you already have."

I can't bear to look up at her. "When does my blood get spilled, ma'am?"

Rezál gives the door a pound. "That's for me to know, and for you to anticipate."

THE ENDGAME

THIRTEEN

I WISH THERE was a different ending here than the one coming. I wish there was a miracle or a trick up my sleeve, something I could pull off in the last possible moment to escape and wreak my vengeance upon the Rule, upon every single person that deserves it. But that was never in the cards.

I spend the next month of my life in the brig, just as Rezál promised, recollecting every single instance where I had gone wrong, where I had doomed myself, and Kaya, and Shay. I track time through the arrival of my dinners. The Third Daughter herself delivers them to me at what I assume to be the end of each day. She never says anything. She simply slides the tray through the small opening in the glass divider between us and watches me eat, sitting cross-legged on the floor. As I eat, I speak to her. At her. I tell her about Kaya and how I taught her the first aerobatics she's ever known. I tell her about Shay and how kind and outgoing he was in basic training. I sing her dirty limericks. She doesn't laugh.

When I run out of heartwarming memories, I tell the Third Daughter about the ten years I've spent trying to leak Rule intel to the breakaways. I tell her about my favourite food delivery service, and how their bots are really cute and always on time. I tell her about how I miss my family and my planetary system, and how generations upon generations of songs, and recipes, and traditions are all gone. I tell her that our first real meeting, one she probably doesn't remember at all, was at Edex during the war games. How, when the drinks were pouring and the still young Rezál wasn't quite sober, Kaya climbed into her lap and entertained her with conversation long after I had gone to sleep. I tell her that I'm not mad about it at all and I understand.

She doesn't come the day after that story. But she returns the next day.

After a few weeks go by, I notice that Rezál has stopped eating. Her already angled face is now gaunt, her eyes shimmer with a feverish glow. "Remember to take your pain medication," I tell her, and she rises from the floor and leaves without an acknowledgement.

I wish I could tell you that the Third Daughter changes her mind and ends the war. But the occasional rumbling of the ship as the shields are hit tells me otherwise. Instead, she pushes forward, harder and harder, engaging in more and more encounters. Usually, I would want to know what her ratios are like, but I don't care anymore.

Then, on the forty-fifth day, the Third Daughter arrives as the cycle begins. Her blues are replaced with a rich cream uniform. Gold trim lines every edge of it from the high collar to the edge of her jacket, just at her thigh. For a few lingering seconds, she watches me through the glass. Her expression is a mixture of sadness, defeat, and resolve.

"The day is here, Ms. Kato," she says, her voice stripped of all its edge.

Two officers in dress uniforms drag me to my feet. "And what's so special about today?"

"Today we win the war." The Third Daughter takes my hands and pushes them slowly behind my back, mindful of the angle that my left shoulder makes. Gently, she clicks the handcuffs in place, but doesn't move. Our chests pressing together, she leans in and whispers, "I have something you can take, so you won't feel anything. You won't be scared."

"I'm not afraid of what's coming."

"There's no need for theatrics," she says, wearily. "No need to suffer more than you have to."

"I think we're well past that, ma'am."

Empires fall. That's a universal law. Where I fail, someone else will succeed, I pray for it every day. I pray for forgiveness. I pray for it now as Rezál escorts me through the sterile corridors of the mothership to the hangar. There, I will spill my blood in the name of the Rule and it will all be for nothing.

"I don't intend to ruin your mood, but what makes you believe you will win today?" I don't really care, but Rezál's voice has a soothing quality to it, at least for me and I want to hear it as much as I can before I die. Even as she leads me to the slaughter, I follow willingly. The Third Daughter makes you feel like the center of the universe.

"You should know," Rezál throws over her shoulder, "you're the one who designed our secret weapon."

My feet stop moving. "Ma'am?"

"Did you really think I stopped work just because I found out about your kill switch? Or did you think I stopped the project because I cared about your wellbeing?" She motions for me to enter the hangar. "Ms. Kato, your implant has worked wonders, even better than expected."

"You...manufactured it?"

The whole hangar is packed with pilots and techs. Rezál leads me through the crowd, her hand resting on the small of my back. I wait for the fear to kick in, for my feet to freeze, but none of it happens. With matched strides we cross the hangar to where the *Morningstar* rests. The fighter gleams solemnly.

"I made modifications. I manufactured it. I trialed it. I shoved your little dragonfly implant into every pilot I could. Did you really think I spent an entire month and half doing nothing?"

I've gone over the moment at least a thousand times, I've visualized every bit of it: the colour of the Third Daughter's uniform, the fighters, the high hangar ceiling. The fear that I was gladly anticipating finally begins to rear its head as I get on my knees before Rezál, before every pilot and tech in the hangar. I've prepared. I know where to look. But nothing prepares me for the way that the hangar lights glisten across the gold, naked blade.

"A sacrifice such as this," Rezál says, voice rising above the crowd, "is rare, but tradition begets it. When the Rule was young and still expanding, fleet engineers would spill their blood to christen a new fighter. Their sacrifice cemented their legacy. Their work. Their pride. Both became part of history, written in blood." Rezál takes a shaky breath. "When we began our work, Ms. Kato demanded that I honour tradition and allow her to spill her blood to bless the victory her technology would aid." She flashes me a sly smile. "And now the day is here."

The hangar erupts in cheers. Rezál raises her hand, and the cheers die immediately. "Ms. Kato has won the war for us, and now, I must honour our agreement."

With heavy steps, Rezál stands behind me. She pulls me flush against her legs, bends down and whispers, "Don't you worry, Nez, I'll make it quick."

"Don't," I push out through clenched teeth. My body shudders against her. "Let me bask in it."

At once, the sharp sting of the blade is against my neck. I close my eyes.

Shay. Kaya. I couldn't protect you. I couldn't take you away from this place. I couldn't forgive you either.

I'm not really here. I'm really still a private, and Shay and Kaya are sleeping on cots beside me. We've been in the bush for ten days and we all smell horribly, and Shay keeps whistling tunes that drive me mad. Kaya is snoring softly. I'll never tell her. I'll never have to now.

I'm not really here, I'm ten and I'm chasing butterflies through the swamps of Oran. The suns are setting. It will be dinnertime soon.

I'm not really here, I'm in bed with Rezál, and it's late, but neither of us wants to go to sleep. She wraps her arms around me and kisses my neck. It's warm under the wool blanket. It's *so* warm. And neither of us knows the taste of blood. Neither of us knows war. We simply live, as different people, in a different place, spared from these parts we're damned to play.

But even in this awful *here*, another day, another hour could change everything. Another dinner, another look at the stars, another story to tell Rezál, another breath. All I want is another breath.

"I don't want to go," I whisper.

I wish I could give you an ending that feels less disappointing. But all I can tell you is that when my eyes open, and the world turns ninety degrees, I'm lying in a spreading pool of crimson. All around me, pilots are dropping. All I can hear are scattered screams. And then, a small voice breaks through it all, a breathy whisper. "How are you doing this? Nez, how is this possible?" Rezál grabs a handful of my hair, but it's too late. It's too late for anything else. I want to tell Rezál that I did the best I could. I held up my end of our contract, I ended the war for her. But it's all over.

The only ending I can give you is the one you already know.

Ennis, if you're listening to this, then the fate of the Rule is already sealed, you've already sacrificed me in the name of the Rule and Mother Eternal, and you've gazed upon the consequences of that sacrifice.

From the beginning, my long game was built on paranoia. You expected the double cross, and I expected you to catch on soon after. We were lying to each other the whole way through; it's the only thing we know how to do. I couldn't leave my kill switch up to chance. Sorry.

I did the only thing any sensible saboteur would do: I made the Rule insert the kill switch for me and gave it no other way out. At the time, Varda thought she was just cramming a shocker into my brain stem, and to anyone looking at the superficial code it would appear exactly so. Anyone who had half a brain to dig deeper would have found the kill switch. Except, how did I know that Varda would wedge the right implant in my head?

I didn't.

I had to make sure that every implant was the right implant. Those shockers aren't made on fleet ships. They're made on a planet three gate jumps from the front lines. I just had to figure out which shipment was going to the mothership and override its base code to embed the kill switch. No, it wasn't as easy as I'm making it out to be, but I got it done.

But Nez, wouldn't that mean that every single person who had the shocker in their brain carried the kill switch and could accidentally, through their own tragic demise, kill every pilot to serve for the Rule? Technically (and practically), no. Just as your retina opens doors on the ships. Just as pilot fighters are calibrated to their bodies. The underlying code of the shocker was designed to only respond to my stress response. No death but my own would trigger it.

No one but a *very frightened* me could trigger the kill switch, since I set the threshold damn high. That's why it was imperative that I be killed. If I died peacefully in my sleep, there was a good chance the switch wouldn't go off.

Ennis, if only you had proceeded with the project as planned, the shocker in my brainstem would be replaced with my dragonfly implant, and you bet your ass I encoded those with the kill switch (which you soon found in the underlying code, *oops*).

And yes, if not for my accident, I could have been beautiful. I could have been your favourite pilot. I could have been a million different things. Instead I became your downfall, a compliment of the highest order. My biggest regret is that our game came to such an abrupt end. I enjoyed it immensely. I enjoyed it more than anything before in my life.

I commit these thoughts to memory, for you, as you march me down the hangar and to my death. For you, as I sit in the brig and count down the days until my execution. Your hand on my waist is so warm. I don't fear what's to come; I know you have a steady hand. I trust you will end my life spectacularly. I trust you.

If I could grant you a farewell wish, it would be that death comes for you swiftly, that there is no pain. That you think of me as it frees your spirit from your aching flesh. I'll wait for you, so that we may continue our game. Whatever that means. Take your time, I'll wait for you no matter how long.

All empires fall, my dear Ennis. It's not personal, it's only natural.

We can both rest now, it's finished.

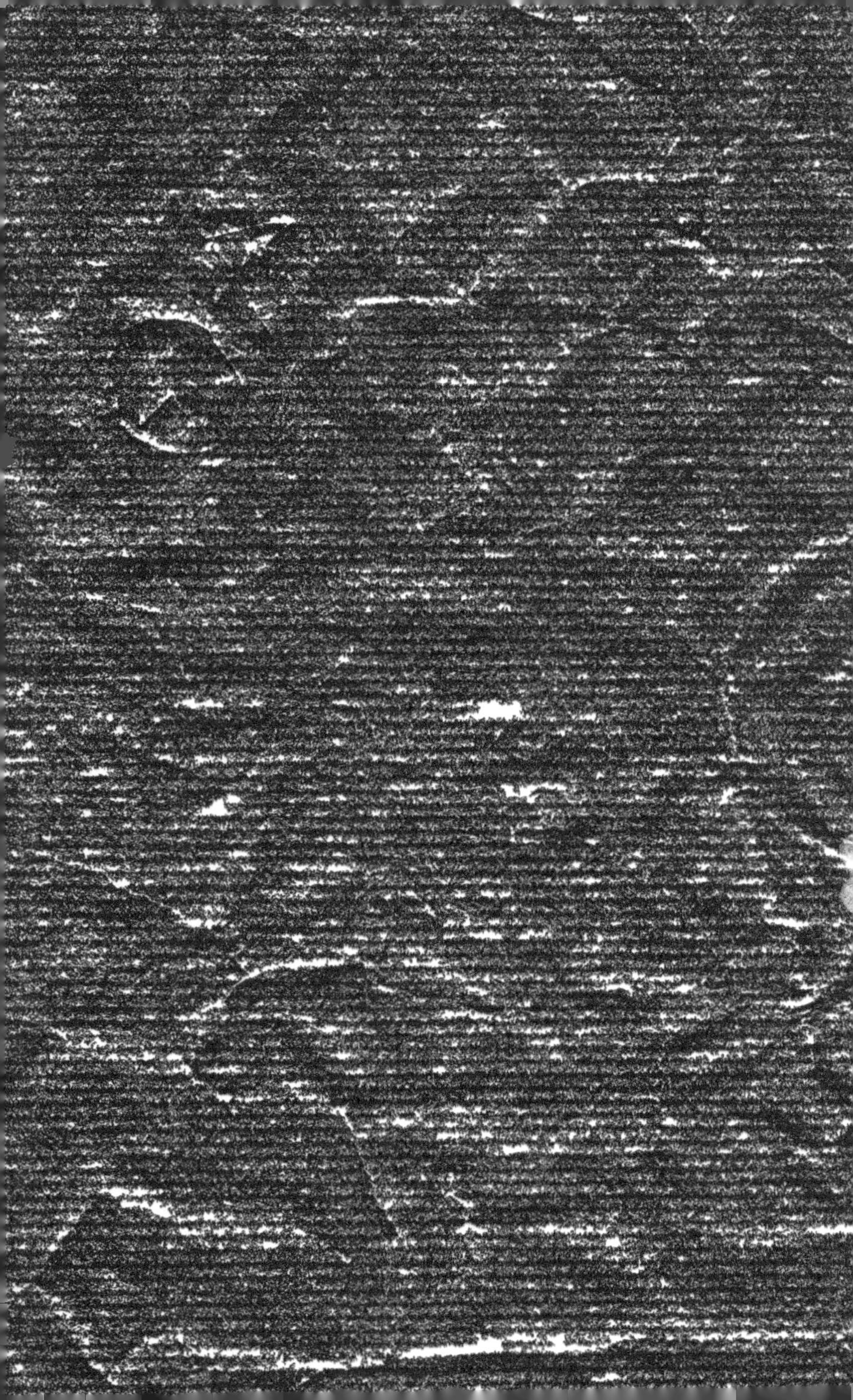

ACKNOWLEDGMENTS

First and foremost, I would like to thank dave ring who read not one, but two on-page executions and decided that it was still the kind of story that he wanted to publish. Thank you, for giving this rage-in-prose a home, and I'm sorry for the COVID-induced, fever dream that was your first read.

No writer exists in a vacuum. And so, I want to thank Eliane Boey, Diana Dima, Pauline Barmby, Yelena Crane, Akis Linardos, Kelsea Yu, and Avra Margariti, who are my closest writing community, who listen to my neurotic ramblings, and often remind me that no, not everyone lives in my head and that I should probably explain some things on page. Elysia Uez, thank you for continually being my first reader and for always noticing the one thing everyone else has missed.

To my partner and the original Sui, Yoah, none of this would be possible without you. I am so proud to share your name. I hope you're proud of what I'm doing with it.

And finally, to the younger me, the eleven, twelve, fifteen-year-old me, we figure things out. It's not pretty, and it's tough going the entire way, and we stumble. But we figure it out. Thank you for holding on, one day at a time. Now, go write the next one.

ABOUT THE AUTHOR

A.D. Sui is a Ukrainian-born, queer, and disabled speculative fiction writer. A failed academic and retired fencer, she spends her days wrangling her two dogs and hundreds of tropical plants. Her writing has appeared in *Dark Matter Magazine, Augur, HavenSpec,* and others. You can find her online at www.thesuiway.com or on any remaining social media platform as @thesuiway.

ABOUT THE PRESS

Neon Hemlock is a Washington, DC-based small press publishing speculative fiction, rad zines, and queer chapbooks. Publishers Weekly once called us "the apex of queer speculative fiction publishing" and we're still beaming. Learn more about us at neonhemlock.com and on social medias at @neonhemlock.